NIGHT SHIFT
Nightriders MC #1

———

SILVER JAMES

Contact: silverjames@swbell.net

Cover design © by Clary Carey, clarycarey@gmail.com

Images: www.depositphotos.com
Handsome Man Portrait ©Subbotina
Motorcycle in flames ©3quarks
Wolf jump illustration ©I.Petrovic

Edited by Gregory Alan

First Print Edition, United States of America
ISBN-13: 978-0-9899217-6-3
ISBN-10: 098992176X

9 8 7 6 5 4 3 2 1

DEDICATION

To everyone who likes to walk on the wild side,
even if it's only from the safety of their favorite
reading spot, with a large cup of coffee (or other
favorite beverage) at their elbow.

ONE

EASY

TROUBLE WALKED THROUGH the door lookin' for me. This sorry excuse for a titty bar, nearly a hundred miles outside of Kansas City, straddled the very edge of the Nightriders' home territory, but the old pervert who owned the place paid us protection and collection money. Or he had. The two fuckers struttin' their stuff toward the bar were askin' for a beat down, and I was ready to hand one out. The bartender flicked his eyes my way. He knew what was comin'. I could handle these boys with my eyes shut. They bellied up to the bar, and I got a good look at their colors.

Fuck. Hell Dogs. What the hell—no pun intended—were they doin' in our territory? These fuckwads needed a geography lesson. We'd heard rumors about them movin' north, but they'd have to be dumb-butt crazy to think they could take us on. As much as I wanted to prove that point, my duty was clear. I needed to get word back to my brothers. Everything in me wanted to beat the shit out of them and haul their stinking carcasses back to the Nightrider clubhouse for some fun and games before we dumped 'em back in their own territory with our patch carved in their skin.

The front door banged open, and five more of the motherfuckers walked in like they owned the place. Shit. I'd been assigned to the night shift—riding Nightrider territory checking out our properties, providing security, and collecting rents. There'd been no whiff of Hell Dog activity on our borders. The Nightriders were national with chapters in every fucking state but here in the Kansas City area? The territory was ours and had been for years. I was tougher than most, but even I couldn't take out that many men.

Discretion was definitely the better part of valor at the moment. I needed to get the hell away so I could contact the MC. Luckily, I was sitting in the very back booth and had a straight shot to the bathrooms and back exit. I'd parked behind the building just in case the local cops cruised by. They fuckin' loved bustin' our asses.

I made it clear of the bar and the parking lot and was about a mile down the highway before I pulled out my cell to phone home. No reception. Figures. I was in Bumfuck, Nowhere. I kicked my Harley into high gear, headed toward the center of Nightriders' territory.

I'd been cruisin' about an hour and figured it was time to check for bars again. I looked at my cell and had a couple. Pulling to the side of the road so I could hear, I hit the button for the clubhouse and listened to the call go through. One of the prospects answered, and I asked for Hardass.

They say you never hear the bullet that kills you. Who the fuck are *they,* and how the hell would they know? They ever been shot? I heard the motherfucker about one second after it blasted a hole through my side. I managed to stay on my bike, and get the hell back on the road, but lost my cell. Running dark on the highway, I laid some fancy moves to lose those bastards trying to kill my ass. Back roads. Tight curves. Didn't matter. They remained on my tail.

Evidently those pussies had pissed on all the road signs to mark their territory. Hardy, the Nightrider vice-president would not be a happy camper when I got back. Because I happened to be wearin' a cut with the right colors, those gawddamned Hell Dogs figured to shoot my ass and ask questions over my dead body. Only I don't die that easy. These bastards were moving into our territory, and I needed to get back to the clubhouse to let the brothers know.

I managed to keep my bike upright for

another ten, maybe fifteen miles—not quite far enough to make it home. I was losin' blood like a stuck pig and laid my bike down trying to take a curve. If I hadn't been half unconscious already, it woulda hurt like a sumbitch.

The five fuckers chasin' me passed by on the road. They wouldn't know I'd crashed for awhile. This part of the road was all up, down, around and through the hills. I needed help but, with no cell phone, had no way to get it. I managed to sit up and look around. I saw lights through the trees and figured that had to be civilization. I dragged my sorry ass through the woods and found a farmhouse. I didn't have much gas left, but I made it to the porch and knocked on the door. Nobody came. I kept hammerin' away, until I passed out. Sort of.

Things went black for a bit, and then I smelled cinnamon rolls and antiseptic. Weird fuckin' combo. A woman leaned over me, and I focused on her face. She looked worried. And scared.

"You're hurt."

"No shit, Sherlock."

"I need to call 9-1-1."

"No."

"But—"

I grabbed her wrist and squeezed. I might be hurt, but I wasn't down for the count yet.

She squeaked and dropped something. It shattered next to my head. A cell phone. Dammit. I could have called the club.

"Get me inside." I gave her arm a shake then let go.

With effort, she helped me to my feet and inside, no easy feat given my size. Or hers. She laid me out face down on a damn table in the kitchen. She went dead still but for her eyes. Damn if they didn't look like she'd been tokin' for a week. She saw my club patch. And recognized it. With a lot of effort, she turned me over and checked my wound.

"Y-you've been shot." She finally blinked a couple of times, inhaled and then looked over her shoulder. "Jonah, go get my kit."

There was a dude here? I pushed up. She pushed down.

"Got it, Mom."

A kid. I relaxed.

I could feel him hovering so I turned my head. He was standing against the wall, big-eyed, and pale. Another kid—a little girl in pigtails—peeked out from behind him.

"This is going to hurt."

"It already fuckin' hurts, babe."

She pressed her lips together and *tsked*. She fucking *tsked*. Who does that besides an old maid school teacher?

Ms. Prim and Proper was wearin' scrubs. Like a nurse. And she had a hellava first aid kit.

"I'm Easy." My real name is Elijah. Elijah Cross. Some asshole decided usin' my initials for my road name would be funny. Since he was the prez of the MC, I damn sure wasn't gonna get in a pissin' match over it. Arguing with the Russian just gets you dead.

"You're a Nightrider." She pointed in the general direction of my 1% patch. That diamond meant the Nightriders were not the good guys. We were outlaws all the way. Her hand fell away and her throat did something funny. Huh. I'd never seen a woman gulp in fear before.

"Yeah. That a problem?"

She gulped again. I watched her throat work, and my damn dick went all stupid. Like the fucker had any chance in hell of getting between those sweet lips.

"Who shot you?"

"Hell Dogs."

The color drained from her face. I'd never seen that either, but damn if that wasn't exactly the way it worked. She was all red-faced one second and completely white the next.

"They can't find you here."

"No shit." I was hangin' on to consciousness by my fingernails. "Call my club. Somebody'll come get me."

She glanced at the front door. The kid

darted that way, squatted down where I couldn't see him. When he came back he held a cell phone—the one that had shattered on the concrete when I made her drop it. "I-I can't. I don't have a land line, only my cell."

"Hip pocket." She'd need my phone for the number.

She eased me over and patted my hip pockets before she tried the front ones. Nothing. Fuck. Now I remembered dropping the thing when I got shot. Could this night get any worse?

"I need to get the bullet out. I-I don't have anything to...I don't have any anesthetic."

Yeah, it could get worse. I'd dumped my bike, lost my phone, and I was bleeding. No fuckin' way was I going to a hospital or back into Hell Dog territory. That still pissed me off. The Russian was not gonna be a happy camper. He, Hardass, and Gravedigger—the inner council—needed to know what was goin' on.

"Just do it."

She did. Watching her face all crinkled up in concentration, I realized she was a pretty woman. She didn't like looking me in the eye, but under the circumstances, not sure I blamed her. I mean, a fuckin' one-percenter shows up on her porch bleedin' like there's no tomorrow, and she has to do surgery on her kitchen table.

Her kid—Jonah—helped. Surprised the hell out of me. Stoic little shit. He fetched and carried without a word. Even brought me a bottle of tequila. She wouldn't let me drink much, said it'd thin my blood and keep it from clotting, but a little would be okay. I ate the damn worm.

Somehow, she got me patched up, back on my feet and climbing stairs to a bedroom on the second floor. Hers from the look of it. She laid me down, and Jonah went to work on my boots. He found both my knife and my hide-out pistol before I remembered they were there. His mom took 'em from him and set them on the table beside the bed.

"Don't touch those, Jojo."

"Is the gun loaded, Mom?"

I managed to mumble, "Yes."

"Okay." He stared at me, blinking like one of those fuckin' owls in that movie about the wizard kid. "I'll make sure Noni doesn't touch it either."

Noni must be the little girl. She was a creeper, staying just out of sight but peeking around corners or her brother.

"It's way past bedtime, sweetie. You and Noni go get ready, and I'll come tuck y'all in."

Pretty Woman had a touch of southern. Reminded me of honeysuckle and sweet tea whenever she talked.

"Do I hav'ta take a bath tonight?"

Her shoulders sort of caved in around her chest as she shook her head. "It's late. You can skip tonight."

"Cool." He peeked around her, grinning at me. "G'night, mister."

Huh. You'd think bloody bikers showed up every night, the way the kid acted. I watched the woman, wondering if maybe that was the case. She'd recognized my colors and the name of the Hell Dogs.

"Uhm...where's your motorcycle? I didn't hear you ride up." She fidgeted and smoothed her hands down her pant legs like her palms were sweatin'.

"Dumped it, back out on the road."

"That explains the road rash. I'll need to debride that soon."

Watching her, I could almost see the thoughts tumbling around in her brain. She finally came to a decision. "The Hell Dogs...will they come looking for you?"

I shrugged, which set off another chain reaction of her thoughts. "Not sure. They'll probably back track, though. My bike's off the road but come daylight, they might see the skid marks."

"I'll go look for it. Try to move it here to the barn or at least hide it out of sight so no one can see it. In case...well, just in case."

"What's your name?"

Her brow crinkled, and her lips did this

little pooch thing. Purse. That was the word. Her lips pursed, and damn if my dick didn't sit up and take notice. Again. Even looking exhausted, with dark circles under her eyes, she was a pretty woman. Blue eyes. Thick lashes. Full lips. And pale blonde hair, sorta silver and gold combined, pulled back in a tail.

"Uhm...you should sleep."

Smart woman, too. Pretty Woman. That's what I called her in my head. PW. I snorted. Yeah, I bet she could pussy whip a man, too.

"So...uhm...I better get going. You know, in case..."

My life was in her hands. She could grab her kids, take off, leave me here. Wouldn't blame her. Frankly? I was too damn tired and hurt to care. "Yeah."

I never heard her leave the house

TWO

EASY

NEAR AS I COULD FIGURE, I was in and out of consciousness for about two days. Sometimes, Pretty Woman was there changing the bandage. Once, the boy was there, offering me water. Everything was sort of hazy—like I was watching the world through a dream. I had the chills. Then I was burning up. I slept. When I woke up, I felt almost human. Well, as human as someone like me can. Because I am almost human. But not quite. I'm a Wolf. We have this crazy-ass gene that lets us shift into wolf form.

I sat up without dying and inhaled. Little kid sweat. Lemon oil. Dryer sheets that pretended to smell like lavender. I ate the soup Jonah brought me. Chicken noodle. From a can. But it was hot and tasted okay. What I really wanted was red meat. Rare.

When the boy came back to get the bowl, he stood there staring.

"What?"

"You gonna stay here long?"

"Just until I can get on my bike and get out

of here."

"Oh." Jonah looked nervous, and he dug the toe of his sneaker against the floor.

"Why? You want me to stay?"

His eyes flicked over my face before he lowered them. "Do you think my mom is pretty?"

What the fuck? I had no clue where this conversation was headed but I'd play along. "Sure. Why?"

"Might you wanna stay and maybe take care of her?"

"Seems like your mom can take care of herself."

He shook his head. "Not really." Jonah darted to the door and looked out before creeping back to stand next to the bed. "Some of the men she gets messed up with? They aren't very nice."

Heh. If the kid thought I was a better alternative, those other men must have been real bastards. "I'm not very nice, kid."

He stared at me long enough that I wanted to bite him or something. "No, you aren't. But you haven't tried to hurt her. Or us."

I heard the front door open and close and so did the kid. He reeked of guilt as he backed out of the room, and I wanted to sneeze to clear my nose of the rotten egg smell. I figured I needed to get the hell out of there as soon as possible. I was in way over my head, and I didn't want to bring trouble to this family. I wasn't a nice guy but I wasn't an asshole. At least not to folks who'd been good to me. I tried to hear the conversation goin' on downstairs but only picked up murmurs. I drifted off before I could figure out what they were talking about.

I woke up and jerked backwards. That creepy little girl was standing next to the bed, staring at me. Noni. The kid never talked—just creeped around and sucked her thumb. She'd never been alone with me, and I wasn't sure what to do. She blinked a couple of times. Her eyes were blue, but a blue so deep it was almost purple. She reached out and I held my breath. A cookie appeared on my bare chest. A vanilla wafer. Shit. I hadn't eaten one of those since I was a kid about her age.

"For me?"

She nodded but didn't say anything. I picked it up and put it in my mouth. She reached out again but this time she poked my cheek with one finger. I stopped chewing and watched. She stuck her finger in her mouth, almost like she was tasting me. It was weird as hell. Then she puckered, kissed her fingertips and laid them on my cheek. My eyes burned for no reason I could figure out and damn if they didn't go all wet when she smiled at me.

When I blinked, Noni turned and slipped out the door. I don't know what the hell had just happened, but it felt like I'd passed some sort of little kid test. It was fuckin' strange but kinda cool at the same time.

I fell asleep—or passed out—still thinking about it. I could have been out five minutes or five hours. I was damn tired of losing time. Then Pretty Woman appeared in the doorway. One eye was black and her lip was split. What the hell?

"You need to leave."

Well, her message was fuckin' plain enough. I'd obviously outstayed my welcome. "Sure." I pushed up and only grimaced a little. I was a lot better. The stitches pulled and itched, but I could breathe and sit at the same time. Progress. "Where are my pants?"

Jonah pushed past her, a pair of jeans in his hands. "These'll fit enough to get you to the car."

"What about my bike?"

He glanced up at his mom and then at me. "It's broken. You'll have to come back. We hid it in the barn out back. Nobody'll find it."

"What's goin' on?" Something bad had gone down. They both stank of ammonia and that meant fear. And Pretty moved funny, like she was having trouble walking.

"You just need to leave, 'kay? We'll get you in Mom's car and take you to wherever you need to go. You can come back later to fix your motorcycle. But you gotta go. Now."

Pretty disappeared, and I heard her clattering down the stairs. I swung my legs over the side of the bed, and Jonah helped by sticking my feet through the legs of the jeans he held. Then he let me lean on him as I stood, pulled 'em up and buttoned 'em. I struggled into a tee shirt the kid held out. My cut was thrown over the footboard. I shrugged into the vest and only grimaced a couple of times.

"What's goin' on, kid?"

He didn't shrug so much as hunch his shoulders but he wouldn't look at me. "You just...you gotta go, mister."

"Easy. My name's Easy."

"Nobody can find you here. We gotta get you back to the Nightriders, 'kay. That's just the way it is."

We got downstairs without breaking our necks. Pretty and the baby were nowhere to be found. Jonah walked me outside. His mom was in the driver's seat of an old beater. Noni was in a car seat thing in the back. I folded into the front seat and buckled the seatbelt. Jonah climbed in back with his sister.

I thought my directions were coherent, but Pretty got lost a couple of times. When we pulled up at the clubhouse, she was pale and her hands white-knuckled where they gripped the steering wheel. Three armed prospects stood at the gate. I got the window rolled down and hollered. They opened up and Pretty drove through.

Gravedigger appeared in front of the car, and she slammed on the brakes. He ripped open the driver's side door and jerked her out, handing her off to the prospects before leaning in the car. He glanced at the kids, his forehead wrinkled up, and then he checked me out.

"Where the fuck you been?"

"Long story."

"The Russian's pissed."

"Figured."

My door opened and Hardass was there to help me out. I glanced into the backseat. "Stay in the car, Jonah. Keep Noni with you."

"What about my mom?" His voice only wavered a little.

Hardy leaned in. "She has to talk to the Russian. She'll be back."

"She'll be fine, kid."

"Promise?" His eyes were the size of half dollars.

"Yeah. I promise."

He studied me for a long moment. "Okay then."

I walked into the clubhouse under my own power, but Hardy stayed close in case I did a face plant. Now that I was up and moving, I felt stronger and almost back to normal. Digger gave one of the prospects instructions to keep Pretty out in the clubroom until the Russian wanted her, and then he ordered the other two back to the gate. He glanced at me.

"We've been on lock down since you disappeared."

I scrubbed at my jaw. Time was still sort of relative. "How long have I been gone?"

"Six days."

"Fuck."

"Yeah." He glanced back at Pretty then opened the massive wooden doors to the room where we held church. He ushered me in, following and shutting the doors behind us. The Russian was there, along with the other officers. You had to be a Wolf to be an officer, but most Nightriders were human. I didn't like the looks on the cadres' faces. Damn. I'd be damn lucky to survive the night.

THREE

JONAH

MOM HAD BEEN GONE FOREVER. With
the car turned off, I couldn't tell how much
time had gone by. Noni needed to pee, and I
knew Mom would be mad if she wet her
pants. I unhooked her and hauled her out of
the car seat. The guys who'd come back out
after Mom went inside were down at the gate
and not paying attention to us. I opened the
door and put my finger to my mouth to shush
Noni. I thought I could sneak her in, find a
bathroom, and get her back outside before
anybody noticed.

I held her hand tight. When we got to the
front door, I worried for a minute that it
might be locked, but it opened when I pushed
on it. There was an entry hall like at school,
and it opened into a huge room. The music
was so loud it made Noni cry. I gave her a
shake and she stopped. I didn't see any doors
out here. We'd have to go into the big room.

I stuck my head around the corner. If I
could find the bathroom door, we'd make a
run for it, and maybe the people in that room

would be too busy to notice. That's when I saw Mom. Three guys had her up on a pool table. There were some women there, laughing and saying bad words. Noni tugged on me. She stood there with her legs crossed and tears in her eyes. I didn't see Easy.

"Hide, Noni." I gave her push and ran into the room. I had to save Mom. I hit one of the guys and grabbed his belt to pull him away. "Leave her alone! Where's Easy? He promised!" I tried to hit him but he shoved me away.

"They're in fuckin' church, you little asshole. We get to play until it's over." The man glanced toward a big wooden door. I jumped up off the floor and ran to it.

EASY

THE RUSSIAN STARED AT ME. I didn't stare back. His looks could be deceptive—all bemused and shit one second, deadly the next. The fucker was a gawddamned genius, and as quick and mean as a viper. He wasn't particularly happy with me at the moment and it showed.

"You have created a problem, Easy. Do you understand what I say?"

"Yeah, I know." A smart man didn't make excuses, just took whatever got dished out. He'd reamed me a new one for dropping out of sight for a week. I made a promise to my ass to get Kevlar boxers if my butt and me made it out of church intact.

"Now tell me."

"I stopped in Barney's to pick up the payment. Got a beer and a burger. Hell Dogs came in like they owned the fuckin' place."

"Did they see you?"

"Didn't think so. I boogied out the back. Fuckin' bartender probably told 'em. Fuckin' Bumfuck, Nowhere. I didn't have any bars on my cell phone. By the time I did, they'd caught up and shot me."

"The woman?"

"I crawled to her house. She's a nurse or something. Fixed me up but I was pretty much out of it."

"She saw your patch?" When I nodded, he added, "If she recognized it, why did she not call?"

"Yeah, about that. I lost my phone when I crashed the bike after I got shot. Broke hers when she tried to get me inside her place. She doesn't have a land line."

Before I could continue her kid burst through the door hellbent to beat the shit out of me.

"You promised!" he screamed. "You promised nobody would hurt her. Not like before."

I didn't move fast enough. The Russian grabbed Jonah by the scruff and held him out at arm's length like the kid weighed no more than a sack of garbage.

"What do you mean *before*?" Jonah kicked and squirmed but couldn't get free. The Russian shook him. "Answer me."

"Before. When those other men came. Lookin' for *him*! They hurt her. They..." All the air whooshed out and the kid wilted. "They did things. Made *her* do things."

"You saw this?"

Jonah grimaced and nodded. "When they came, she told me to get Noni and hide. Told us we couldn't make a peep. No matter what. That as long as we were quiet, we'd be safe." His eyes cut my way. "He'd be safe."

Well, fuck. That explained the bruises I'd seen. And other shit. Like the way she walked, sort of shuffling like something was broken. The Hell Dogs had come looking, found her alone, and being Dogs, they raped her. I felt sick. Like puke up my guts sick. She didn't give me up. I'd slept through the whole damn attack, too weak to do a fuckin' thing to help her. I owed her now, even though we'd all be dead if she'd said anything. She was smart enough to know that.

I found my voice. "What about Noni?"

A tear slipped from his eye, and he brushed it away with the back of one hand. "I covered her eyes and mouth. She was crying. We hid in the cupboard 'cuz we didn't have time to get out of the house and hide in the cellar."

"Why do you come in here?" The Russian shook Jonah again.

"Those men. Out there. They're...they're ...doin' stuff to my mom." His eyes found me again. "You promised when she said she'd bring you here. You promised nobody would hurt her or us. That you'd get out and go away and we'd be safe. But we're not." He started kicking and swinging again. "Let me go. I have to help my mom!"

Well, fuck. I pushed to my feet but the Russian was already through the door, Hardy and Gravedigger right on his ass. We trooped into the clubroom and sure 'nuff, three of the prospects had Pretty Woman pinned spread-eagled on the pool table. They'd stripped off her jeans. Two of the club whores watched, smirking. I wanted to slap those bitches. Instead, I went for the asshole holding his dick between Pretty's legs. Digger and Hardy went for the other two.

I hauled the guy off and felt something rip in my side. I didn't give a shit. I wanted to pound the bastard into a greasy pile of shit.

"You gawddamn motherfucker!" I tore into the prospect, and he punched me in the mouth.

"What the fuck, asshole! She's not wearing a property patch. The bitch was standing here and she didn't say no."

My claws itched to come out, and I was primed to rip the fucker's throat out. Instead, I tossed him against the wall. The back of his head connected with the open mouth of the Wolf pelt we had hanging on the wall. That old Wolf might be dead and skinned but he was still a motherfucker. One of his canines ripped open the back of the prospect's head. The scent of hot blood mixed with sweat, fear, and lust. I took a step toward the asshole.

"Enough."

The word came out all quiet-like, but every last one of us knew the Russian meant business. I glanced over and almost lost my hold on the fuckwad I was ready to kill. The Russian held Jonah, the kid's face planted against his chest so the boy couldn't see what was happening to his momma. Jonah's arms were wrapped around the Russian's neck with his legs clamped around the big man's waist. I was glad the kid couldn't see the Russian's face and was double damn happy I wasn't one of those prospects. I glanced at Gravedigger. He'd have work to do before the night was done.

Something sticky dribbled along my side, and I glanced down. A bright red splotch stained my tee shirt. Yeah, I'd torn open the stitches. When I quit being pissed off it was gonna hurt like a sumbitch. A couple more members rushed in. Two of 'em grabbed the guy I was holding. I looked over at the pool table. PW had curled up in a fetal ball. I picked her up, and my heart almost shredded at her whimper.

"Shhh, darlin'. It's me. It's Easy. I'm not gonna hurt you."

She quieted as I carried her over to the Barracks. Adrenaline still ran hot inside me so she felt light. I had a room in the other building, one nobody fucked with. I laid her on my bed and threw a blanket over her. Footsteps shuffled behind me, and I whirled, ready to deck whoever was stupid enough to follow. It was Sunny, one of the old ladies. She held PW's jeans and shoes.

"Can I help, Easy?" She glanced at the bed and winced. "Repo and I walked in after it was over. He's going with Digger. I followed you."

Sunny was Repo's property and a sweet thing, all bright like her name. Pretty would probably feel better with another woman around. I nodded to Sunny, and she sat down on the bed. "Hey, sugar. My name's Sunny. You're gonna be okay now. Easy and I'll take care of you."

Pretty opened her eyes and fixed on me. I could barely swallow the rage burning in my gut as I choked out the question. "Why didn't you tell me?"

She dropped her gaze. "What difference

24

would it make?"

"It makes a big damn difference. Trust me." I swallowed the bile in my throat and reached for the blanket. "I don't wanna embarrass you, but I gotta see, babe. I gotta see what those Hell Dog fuckers did to you."

I pulled the blanket back, and opened her knees. I thought I was ready. I wasn't. Bruised flesh, cuts, her pussy so swollen I didn't know how she could walk at all. "Fuck."

"Yes," she murmured. "They did."

"No, babe. What they did was rape. And they'll pay. I promise." Those last words rang a little hollow. I'd made a lot of promises to Pretty and her kids. So far, I hadn't kept one of them.

"Would you like to take a bath?" Sunny leaned closer, pulling attention to herself.

Pretty nodded.

"Okay. I'll run one for you and find some clean clothes that will fit."

All the sudden, Pretty came up off the bed, whites showin' around her eyes. "Jojo! Noni!"

I grabbed her and glanced at Sunny. I knew Jonah was okay. Well, as okay as a kid could be with the Russian. I'd totally forgotten about Noni. "I'll find her. Take care of the Pretty Woman, Sunny."

Out in the clubroom, I found Jonah sitting on the bar eating a bowl of ice cream with the Russian. That stopped me dead in my tracks.

Who knew the Russian might have a soft streak?

"Not a word, Easy." Hardy nudged me in the back. "I need to look at your wound."

I nodded absently. Hardy was our medic. He'd been one for real and saw combat in Afghanistan. "In a minute. I gotta find Noni." As soon as I said her name, Jonah almost dropped his bowl. The kid went white and looked as guilty as Cain. He made to jump off the bar, but the Russian wrapped him up with an arm around the kid's waist.

"Noni?"

"My sister." Jonah looked close to bawlin' again. "I told her to go hide when...when..."

The Russian cut him off so the kid didn't have to say the words. "We will find her."

Took us close to twenty minutes, even with our noses. The little dickens had hidden in the very back of one of the kitchen cabinets. She only came out when Jonah crawled in after her. She didn't cry. She didn't scream. In fact, she didn't do anything but stare at us, with those big ol' blue eyes of hers. She didn't even whimper when the Russian picked her up, but she didn't relax either.

"Tell the mother they are fine."

The kid stared at the Russian with those innocent blue eyes of hers. "I have to go peepee," she whispered.

That was my clue to skedaddle. When I got

back to my room, Pretty was dressed. Her clothes had been ripped so she wore one of my tees and a pair of jeans belonging to one of the old ladies. She sat on the edge of my bed, hands clasped between her knees as Sunny combed out her wet hair.

Both of them looked up at me, and I think I smiled. "Kids are fine, babe. They're havin' ice cream."

Hardy followed me in, first aid kit in hand. That's when Pretty Woman noticed the blood.

"You're hurt again."

I shrugged. "Yeah. I probably ripped the stitches when I—" Hardy nailed me in the back with his elbow, and I clamped my jaw so fast I almost bit my tongue.

She nodded, but none of us missed the shudder that ran through her. "I..." She inhaled and let her breath out slowly. "Give me a minute then I'll fix it." Her hands were shaking so hard there was no way she could do anything.

"I got this, sugar." Hardy pushed me into a chair and knelt beside me. He went to work without another word. It was one reason he and I got along. Neither of us was much for talkin' about shit. We'd rather do. At the moment, I really wanted to *do*. I wanted to find those motherfuckin' Hell Dogs. When I got my hands on them, I'd make damn sure they suffered for what they'd done to Pretty

Woman. And I planned on ripping off the heads off those Nightrider prospects. They were dead meat and their whores with them.

FOUR

JONAH

I HEARD MOTORCYCLES. For a minute, I thought maybe it was Easy and the Nightriders. They'd taken care of Noni and me and Mom, and after a couple of days, we got to come home. Easy said they'd come out soon to pick up his motorcycle. That was two weeks ago. I looked out the window but didn't recognize the men riding in circles in the front yard. Then I caught a glimpse of the back of one vest. Cut. Easy called his vest a cut. The patch showed a dog with horns. Hell Dogs. I knew the guy parked right in the middle of them. The Bastard had found Mom. I had to get us out the back door, get us hidden until they left.

Noni was in her room playing tea party with her stuffed bear. I grabbed her and dragged her downstairs. Mom was trying to call someone on her new cell phone.

"Hide, baby," she hissed. "Take Noni and hide. No matter what happens, don't come out."

I didn't want to leave Mom, but it was up to me to take care of Noni. If the Bastard got his hands on my sister, bad stuff would happen to her. Really bad stuff. That's why Mom had gotten Aunt Sam to help us hide. We'd been safe for almost a year. Until Easy showed up. They'd found us because of him. I grabbed Noni's coat and put it on her, then grabbed mine.

"Jojo, after they leave, you have to go. You and Noni will need help. Go to Easy. He'll take care of you."

I wanted to argue. This was all Easy's fault, but Mom was right. The Nightriders hated the Hell Dogs. They'd keep Noni safe. "Mom?"

"Go, baby. I'll be fine. Don't let them find you."

Noni didn't want to leave. I had to pick her up and carry her out the back door. There was a cellar back behind the barn. Mom had cleaned it up. Put water and cookies and a flashlight in it. In case of storms, she'd said, but I knew it was in case we needed to hide. I took Noni there and we got inside. I closed the door and bolted it, just like Mom taught me. She'd come. After those men left. Mom would come to get us, and everything would be okay.

Noni finally fell asleep. I turned off the flashlight to save batteries and sat on the steps right beneath the door. I couldn't hear anything. No yelling. No engines. I was scared, like pee-in-my-pants scared. Bad things would happen to us if Mom didn't come. The Bastard would get ahold of Noni. And my old man... I didn't want to think about him. He was a cop, but he beat Mom and me. He'd have a bad day, come home, get drunk, and he'd start in on her. She tried to get divorced, but nobody believed he beat her because he was a cop and stuff.

Then she hooked up with the Bastard. Everything was good for awhile. He made sure my old man stayed away from us. Then Mom got pregnant. He started bringing other girls around. They were younger than Mom, like barely out of high school. And they had tattoos and didn't wear many clothes. One of them came into my room one night and wanted to do stuff. I was embarrassed and told her to go away. The Bastard caught her, but thought it was funny.

He didn't hang around the house as much after Noni was born. At least when she was a baby. After she could walk, he started hanging around again. I'd grab Noni and we'd go to the neighbor's house. That always pissed the Bastard off. He came one night when I was asleep. I woke up and heard Noni crying. I went to check on her and found him in her room, touching her. I hit him with my baseball bat. That's when Mom called Aunt Sam, and she came to get us. We lived with her in Utah for a couple of months, but Mom got homesick. She didn't like the snow and mountains so we came back here. Mom had been a nurse in Kansas City, but she couldn't work in the hospital anymore because either my old man or the Bastard would find us. She worked in a crappy place with a bunch of old people, but they paid her cash and she didn't have to use her real name.

Way too much time had gone by and still no Mom. I needed to go check, but I didn't want Noni to go with me. I couldn't leave her in the cellar by herself. Maybe I could sneak her into the barn, hide her up in the loft. But...I was scared she'd fall down the ladder and get hurt. I had no choice. I'd just have to take her with me. She didn't want to wake up so that sort of made things easier. If she was asleep, she wouldn't wander off. I could look for Mom then come back and get her. I left Noni alone while I went to check the house.

Mom wasn't there. Neither was anyone else. All we could do was wait. I woke up Noni, made her come into the house, and fed her some cereal with the last of the milk. Mom hadn't been to the store so there wasn't much left to eat. I didn't know how long Noni and me could wait.

🐾🐾🐾🐾

THREE DAYS WENT BY and Mom hadn't come home. We still didn't have a phone at the house. Easy bought Mom a new cell, which I figured she'd taken with her—so she couldn't call to tell me what to do. Just in case, I looked for it but the phone was gone. I needed to call Aunt Sam but I had to get to a phone. There was a gas station out on the road a couple of miles away. I could walk there pretty fast, but I couldn't leave Noni. We didn't have any more food so I had no choice. I made Noni wear her warm coat and let her take her stupid bear. Maybe she wouldn't fuss so much if she had it with her. Holding her hand, I started down the driveway. That's when I heard the motorcycles.

Dragging Noni into the woods, I left her hidden in the bushes while I snuck back to see what was going on. Hell Dogs pulled into our yard and drove around making donuts in what was left of the grass. Then I saw Mom's car. Things were gonna be okay now. Mom was back. As it drove by, I realized the Bastard was driving. When the car stopped, two guys went to the passenger door and pulled Mom out. She didn't fight them. She didn't move at all.

This was bad-bad-bad. Mom was hurt something awful. Even if we got to the gas station, I couldn't call the cops. They wouldn't do anything. And my old man might find us. Easy. Mom told me to call him. I'd figure out how to find Easy and the Nightriders. He told Mom he owed us. They had to come help.

EASY

WHEN THE PROSPECT called up from the gate, the last thing I expected to hear was that a deputy sheriff was down there asking for me—by my real name. And he didn't have a warrant. Digger and Hardy exchanged looks and followed me out the door. The prick stood there all puffed up and official looking trying his best to stare down the boys guarding the gate. One of 'em was a Wolf. Deputy Dawg wasn't gonna win that pissin' contest in this lifetime.

I sauntered up to the gate and stopped about three feet back from it. "Whaddaya want?"

The deputy looked me up and down then jumped when the passenger door on his cruiser opened. Jonah climbed out. Before anyone could move, the kid rushed the gate.

"Dad!"

Dad? He was callin' me *dad*? What the fuck?

Deputy Dawg grabbed the kid and hauled him back. "Not so fast. You Elijah Cross?"

I didn't use my real name very often, but I nodded. "Yeah. Jonah, what's goin' on?"

The kid squirmed, trying to jerk free from the cop. Somebody banged on the back window of the cruiser and I heard Noni screaming. "What the hell? Is that Noni?"

Jonah did his best not to cry. Fuck. There was something really bad wrong here. "Open the fuckin' gate," I ordered. Stepping through, I jerked Jonah away from the deputy and headed to the car. I wrestled the door open and Noni fell into my arms, wailing and clutching that dumb bear she dragged everywhere.

"These kids belong to you?" The deputy got all surly, and he kept his hand on the butt of his pistol.

I didn't know what game Jonah was playing, but after seeing at how dirty the kids were, I figured it was better to get them inside first and find out later. "Yeah. They're mine. Why?"

"Caught 'em hitchhiking on Old Centervale Road. Kid said his mom took off with a boyfriend and told 'em to go visit you."

I stared at Jonah. He stared back, his face pale. He reeked of ammonia. Not just fear but terror. Bad shit had happened to Pretty Woman. I knew it in my gut. I hitched Noni on my hip and clutched Jonah's shoulder, pulling him closer to the gate. "It's my week for visitation. The asshole she's with doesn't always let her drop the kids off." I lied through my teeth and felt Jonah relax slightly.

Deputy Dawg didn't want to surrender the kids. He kept fingering the butt of his pistol. I nudged Jonah closer to the gate. Once we were on the other side, Dawg couldn't do much. I challenged him. "You gotta problem? I pay my child support. Ain't my fault my ex sucks at pickin' boyfriends."

"You sure this is where you want to be, boy?"

Jonah leaned against me and nodded. "Yes sir. My dad'll take care of us. He always does."

Noni picked that moment to pat my cheeks. "Hungry. Nilla cookie, 'kay?"

"Sure, baby. I'll get you some."

The deputy relaxed slightly, but I kept edging back toward the gate. As soon as Jonah was close enough, Hardy grabbed him and hauled him through. I was a step behind and the gate clanged shut the moment I was on the inside. I glanced back. "Thanks for bringin' 'em, deputy. I'll take care the kids now."

The dude wasn't a happy camper, but I could see him working out alternatives. Noni patted me again. "Da! Cookies!" Her demand seemed to settle the deputy. He nodded and retreated to his car, though he didn't leave until we'd gone inside.

Sunny was waiting in the foyer. She grabbed Noni and headed toward the kitchen.

Jonah started to follow, but I stopped him.

"What's goin' on, kid? Where's your mom?"

He squared his shoulders, and I noticed his hands were fisted at his sides. "The Hell Dogs came back. Mom told us to hide in the cellar. I waited a long time, but she never came." He swallowed and stared down at his feet. "I should have gone to look sooner, but when I did, she was gone. They were gone."

"When was this?"

He gulped and still wouldn't look at me. "Three days ago. I decided to take Noni to the gas station so we could call you. There wasn't any more food." He looked up then, and his eyes looked haunted. "We were halfway down the driveway when I heard the noise. The Hell Dogs came back. Noni and I hid in the woods. They...Mom didn't move when they pulled her out of her car. I knew something was bad wrong. I grabbed Noni and we ran. The deputy pulled up right before we got to the station. He made us get in his car. I made up the story about you bein' our dad so he'd bring us here."

"Are the Hell Dogs still at your house?" The Russian had come up beside me, and I hadn't even noticed.

Jonah nodded, his eyes huge. "Yeah. I guess. They didn't look like they were in any hurry to leave."

The Russian stared at me. "Can you find

the way back?"

I had to think about that. I could get close but I wasn't sure of the exact location. I'd find the place, but it might take awhile. The Russian knew just by looking at me that I was waffling.

"Jonah, you will show us the way. Repo, take Easy and the boy in the truck. We will need to get Easy's ride while we are there. Everyone else, mount up."

FIVE

EASY

I WANTED JONAH to stay in the truck. We'd
stopped about half a mile away from Pretty
Woman's house. Hollywood slipped into the
woods to shift into his wolf so he could scout
the situation. He wasn't gone long.

"Place is empty. They've been gone about
thirty minutes. Maybe an hour. So many
scents overlaying the place it's hard to tell."
Hollywood glanced at the truck, and his eyes
slid away from making contact with Jonah's
gaze. "The woman's there. In the yard. It ain't
pretty, Russki."

The Russian nodded and looked
contemplative, like he already knew the
score. "Where is Easy's Harley?"

"In the barn back behind the house,
covered in hay, just like the kid said. Those
fucking Dogs didn't find it. There's somethin'
else goin' on here, boss."

"Ya think?" I was all snarly, but fuck, I
figured I was entitled.

The Russian gave me one of his looks so I
shut up. I was still pissed though. I'd made

39

promises. We were royal assholes, but a promise was a promise.

The Russian called over the brother standing next to the pickup. "Repo, take the boy and the truck to get the Harley. See that the boy packs some clothes for the children, but do not let him see the front yard. Leave as little trail as possible."

Repo nodded, one short jerk of his chin. "You got it, Russki."

Hollywood pointed toward the trees lining the highway. "There's a dirt cutoff about a hundred yards up the road. You can use it to get to the barn. Nobody'll see tracks."

Repo climbed in, and I watched him explain things to Jonah. The kid looked a little panicked, but he manned up. Little dude impressed the hell outta me.

"Ride with me, Easy." The Russian rode his bike like he was fused to the metal, and I wasn't about to argue about riding the bitch seat. We rolled up the driveway, our tire tracks mixing with the ones already there. Hollywood was right. The Hell Dogs were long gone, but Pretty Woman remained, laid out in the yard like a fucking pagan sacrifice. The shit they did to her was obscene. Fuck. We were Wolves. We did bad shit, but leave it to a human to do evil like this. Russki was pissed, especially when he got a look at the message carved into her stomach.

Noni is mine. Bring her to me.

What the fuck? Noni was what? Three? Maybe four? I glanced at the Russian, and his gaze flicked over to meet mine. Red flecks flickered in the back of his eyes. Shit. He was about to go furry. I'd never seen Russki lose control of his wolf. I stepped back, as did every other Nightrider who was a Wolf. A few of the humans stood there like deer in headlights. Power rolled off the Russian, and my own wolf got a little twitchy. I stuffed him down inside because I damn sure didn't want to be prey. Still, the question had to be asked.

"What do you wanna do, Russki?"

"The children are under my personal protection."

I nodded. That meant every Nightrider in the whole fuckin' country would lay down their lives for Jonah and Noni. Since this was in line with my own promises to Pretty Woman, I was squarely on board with that.

"We need answers, boss."

"Yes. If Jonah does not have them, we will find them somewhere else."

"The kid mentioned an aunt."

The Russian continued to stare at Pretty Woman, and I wondered if he'd heard me. After a long, few minutes, he nodded. "He will call her when we get back to the clubhouse. She will come. She will have the answers we need."

I didn't want to ask the next question."

"What about Pretty?"

"We must leave her. Let the police find her." He raised his head, sniffed the air. "We will need to leave Hell Dog evidence before they do."

That made sense. The bike tracks were obvious, even to the lazy cops in this town. We'd be the obvious suspects since this was our territory.

Russki stared at the letters carved into her skin. "And we must erase that. You said the Dogs have taken over Barney's."

"Yeah, pretty much."

His lips curled, but I wouldn't call the expression a smile. It meant someone was going to die.

"Gravedigger, take four others."

Digger grinned, but his eyes promised nothing but death. "On it, boss." He whistled, and two prospects mounted their bikes. Hollywood and Wizard climbed on theirs. They roared off into the night.

The hair on the back of my neck prickled. I damn sure wouldn't want to be a fuckin' Hell Dog tonight. The pack was hunting. I was just sorry it wasn't me riding with 'em. I still wasn't a hundred per cent though most of my wounds had scabbed over. As wolf shifters, we healed faster than humans, but it wasn't immediate, and we weren't immortal or any of that movie shit. I heard the truck start up around back. Repo would be headed back to the clubhouse with Jonah and my bike.

As if reading my mind, Russki moved to his ride. "Easy," he commanded.

I climbed on behind, and he kick-started the engine. We rolled down the drive. When we hit the road, the others lined up in riding formation. We caught up to the truck and followed it back to town.

We had a garage and body shop set up in an old train maintenance building next to the Barracks, and I headed that way to help unload my bike. This was the first time I'd seen it since the wreck. Fuck. It needed almost a total rebuild. Repo looked like he wanted to slap me upside the head.

"What were you thinkin', boy?"

"I was thinkin' I'd been fuckin' shot and the dickwads were hot on my trail." I walked over and leaned against the truck-bed railing. "Is it as bad as it looks?"

"Won't know 'til I get it down and apart. Definitely needs body work. I think the engine will be okay." He cut his eyes to Jonah, who sat in the cab with the passenger door open. "You ever used tools, boy?"

The kid's eyes went round. "No, sir."

Repo laughed. "You're too damn polite, kid. My name is Repo. Use it. I'm gonna need some help on this bike. You think you can do the work?"

"Yes, sir...er...Mister Repo."

Repo rolled his eyes at me. "Close enough. Go with Easy and settle in. Get cleaned up and get a night's sleep. We'll start work first thing in the morning."

The kid slid out of the truck, quivering like a puppy waiting on a belly rub. "Yes, sir, Mister Repo. I'll be here."

I steered the kid away before Repo jumped him again for being too polite. Pretty Woman had done a good job with her kids. Had to be hard, bein' a single mom and all. The words carved into her body flashed in my mind. We needed to get to the bottom of that, but first things first.

"You said you have an aunt?"

"Yeah. She's in the mountains. Colorado or Utah or someplace like that."

The kid was hedging. He didn't want to tell me exactly where this aunt lived. I'd deal with that later. "The Russian wants you to call her, tell her to come."

He stopped and got real still. I turned around, and the kid wouldn't meet my eyes. Head down, he dug his toe in the dirt. "That means Mom's gone."

Had he figured it out? I stalled by asking, "Gone?"

"Did she take off with the Bastard again?"

Fuck. If only it were that simple. How did I

tell him that his momma was dead, and we'd just left her laying there in the dirt? "Tell me about this bastard."

Jonah glanced up and stared at me. I could see the war going on in his brain, and I caught whiffs of ammonia. Whoever the sumbitch was, he scared Jonah. "He's not *a* bastard, he's *the* Bastard. Like that's his name or something. He's this guy Mom hooked up with. He promised to take care of us, but..." He looked down, digging in his toe again.

"What's he to Noni?"

His head jerked up and gulped. "Nothing. He's just some guy." Jonah's scent changed to rotten apples—sickly sweet over a base of decay. The kid was fucking lying to me. Now why the hell would he do that? Either he'd tell me or the Russian would get it out of him. Instead of pushing, I handed him my cell. "Call your aunt. Tell her she needs to get her ass here. Now. Your mom ain't coming back."

SIX

EASY

AS I WALKED DOWN to the gate, Hardy and
Digger trailed behind me by about two steps.
No one woke up Jonah to tell him his aunt
had arrived. The prospects on guard duty
looked jumpy. A bad-ass Jeep rigged to run
was parked smack damn in the middle of the
drive in front of the gates. The woman
leaning against its front bumper looked like
hell on wheels. Short, spiky blonde hair, old-
style fatigues, combat boots, and a fuckin'
semi-automatic pistol strapped to her hip.
She was long and lean and would put a man
in mind of some hot sex if it weren't for her
grim expression.

That's when I stopped dead in my tracks. I
knew she was Pretty Woman's sister but holy
hell. This woman was Pretty's evil twin. No,
seriously. Add some curves and long hair, and
I'd be lookin' at Pretty. It was a weird fucking
feeling. But this woman was hard. Everything
about her.

"I'm Easy."

"And I'm not. Where're my kids?"

"They're not yours."

"The hell you say. Jonah and Noni are mine. That's the way Sarah wanted it."

Sarah. So that had been her name. At the moment, she was a Jane Doe in the morgue. We'd gathered up the kids' stuff and got the hell out after we discovered her body. Digger and some of the brothers went hunting, and they left Hell Dog evidence behind—blood, a torn cut, and the house burning to cover our tracks. An anonymous call alerted the local authorities, and they swarmed the place. Interacting with cops usually meant one or more of us in jail for the duration.

After he called her, Jonah wouldn't tell us his aunt's name. Hell, we couldn't get his mother's name or their last names out of him. Probably just as well. It'd be pretty damn stupid for any of us to ID his mother. So far, that fuckin' deputy who'd dropped off the kids hadn't put two and two together and come back looking for them. Our luck wouldn't hold indefinitely.

I stopped and crossed my arms over my chest while I studied the woman. She didn't seem nervous. That wasn't too smart on her part. I glanced at the weapon on her hip. "Why don't you put your gun away, come inside, and we'll talk."

"I have a better idea. Why don't y'all bring my nephew and niece to me and the three of us will just mosey on outta here."

"Not gonna happen. Not tonight. They're already asleep." Stupid bitch. It was pushin' midnight. We stared at each other. I blinked first, but then I always do. Doesn't mean I'm gonna back down. I stepped closer to the gate just as somebody up at the clubhouse hit the switch for the floodlight, spotlighting her. She didn't move. I gave her credit for that, but I had a good look at her now. Dark circles under red, puffy eyes. The hand she had hooked in her belt shook slightly. She was exhausted and scared, but doin' her damnedest not to show it. I inhaled, caught her scent. Damn if my dick didn't perk right up even though she looked like death warmed over. What was up with that? I shifted my feet to give my dick a little more room in my jeans.

"What's your name?"

Her eyes narrowed, and her nose did this little twitchy thing as she pressed her lips together. My dick liked that a lot. It was makin' plans to get between those lips with that cute little nose buried in my groin while I came in her mouth.

"Y'all don't need to know."

"Yeah, babe, we do. You want to see the kids, we need to know your name."

Her nose squiggled again. "Fine. I'm Sam Prescott."

"Sam?"

"Short for Samantha, okay?" She thrust her chin at me. "Did you murder Sarah?"

Why did she automatically assume Pretty was dead, much less murdered? Jonah only told her Pretty—Sarah—was gone and to come. Still, she was gutsy to ask that question. I answered honestly. "No."

"The only way she'd leave the kids is if she's dead. If you didn't kill her, who did?"

"We're not sure." Okay, I hedged a bit. We knew. Mostly. And I wouldn't straight up lie to her about this.

"But you have an idea. That's good enough for me. Tell me who the hell killed her."

Her right hand barely moved but her palm now cupped the butt of her pistol. Put me in mind of someone gettin' ready to make a statement. Then another idea hit me. Maybe she was gonna turn all vigilante or some stupid shit like that. "You goin' huntin' for who did her?"

"Maybe." Her mouth twisted into something that might be a smile.

"How long you been drivin'?"

Her left shoulder lifted slightly. "'Bout twenty hours."

"Put the pistol in your Jeep. Someone'll park it around back. Come up to the clubhouse, get something to eat. You can look in on the kids, prove to yourself they're okay.

We'll find a place for you to bunk for tonight."

Digger stepped up beside me, arms loose at his sides. "Or you can sit out here 'til morning. You still won't see the kids as long as you're wearing that."

I shot Digger a look. He didn't know when to shut up, and he had his Beretta out and hidden behind his leg. If she so much as twitched, she'd be dead. I'd seen Digger work up close and personal. He was as quick as a rattlesnake and twice as deadly.

"Y'all put yours down, I'll put mine away." She called Digger's bluff, eyes flicking down for just a second.

Damn but she was cold. Her eyes hadn't left me until that quick glance, but she knew he had a gun all but trained on her. For all that she looked like Pretty Woman—Sarah— she was the polar opposite. Sarah had been honeysuckle and sweet tea. Her sister was all steel magnolia. The bitch looked like she could cut off a man's balls, roll 'em in batter, and deep fry those suckers. Hell, looking at the fire spittin' from her eyes, she'd more likely just hit 'em with some hot sauce and eat those puppies raw.

"Truce," I suggested, holding my hands out. "Nobody will bother you. Or your stuff."

"Your word."

"You have *my* word."

Fuck. When did Russki sneak up on us?

She must have figured out he was the man in charge because she straightened, pushed off the bumper, and walked around to the driver's door. Digger wasn't hiding his Beretta any longer. She took off the holster and belt, opened the door and tossed her weapon on the passenger seat. Digger's pistol disappeared into the back waistband of his jeans.

"Okay." She pulled out a backpack, slung it over one shoulder and tossed her keys through the gate to one of the prospects. "You scratch her, I'll take it out of your hide."

She brushed past me and I caught another hint of her scent—vanilla, cedar, and something more elusive. My wolf sat up, panting and thumping his tail. What the fuck? I wanted to bury my nose in her hair and just breathe. Hardy nailed me between the shoulder blades.

"What's with you?" he muttered.

Not Sam. But she would be.

SAM

WHAT IN THE HELL was I thinking? Oh, wait. I wasn't, obviously. Ever since Jonah called to tell me Sarah was gone, I'd been in a flat out panic. Did the Bastard find her? We'd taken such pains to keep her and the kids out of sight. And I wanted to know how she got messed up with another outlaw motorcycle gang. I'd never be able to ask her now. I was dead on my feet, but these assholes weren't leaving me any options.

The dudes at the gate were puppies. The three who'd come to meet me were the real deal but the fourth guy? He was holy-shit-I'm-gonna-die scary. If I read the crap on his cut right, he was the man in charge. El Presidente. He was foreign, but I couldn't quite identify the accent. Eastern Europe, maybe. I damn sure didn't want to be left alone in a room with the man. He looked all benign and maybe not too bright at first glance, but I could see it in his eyes. A predator, for sure and for certain. The same with tall-dark-and-scruffy. He'd been holding a pistol from the moment he saw I was armed. They called him Gravedigger. I did *not* want to know how he got his road name.

All of them were big. Tall, broad, muscled. And tats. Why did bikers need to ink their skin? I studied the other two, who looked almost sweet in comparison to the president and the killer. Almost. These guys were deadly and no matter how hot they looked, I couldn't forget that fact. They all wore black leather cuts, the fronts covered with small patches detailing their pedigrees. The backs showed a three-piece patch. The top rocker said NIGHTRIDERS which curved over the graphic of the front half of a leaping wolf, the back half trailing off into a stylized comet-like tail. The bottom rocker said ORIGINAL. Crud. This was their national chapter house. All I could think was "frying pan—fire."

The guy in the lead looked me up and down. I returned the favor. Full tattoo sleeve on one arm—colorful even in the dim light, brownish hair cropped short on the sides and longer on top. What the heck was up with that? Tall, broad-shouldered, tapered hips, and I caught a whiff of leather and motor oil. His face looked like the boy next door's until I caught the glint in his eyes. Blue. As blue as the Siberian husky who lived at the lodge where I worked ski patrol. But feral. Wild. He might look all aw-shucks, but he was a predator, too.

Crud. He grinned and twin dimples creased his cheeks. Yeah, he was easy all right. So easy the club girls would be all over him like bar-b-que sauce on smoked ribs, and I bet he tasted just as good. He had a killer grin. I reminded myself of that adjective. Killer. He wore the patch and everything. He'd be a killer in bed too, as my libido happily informed me. I reminded said libido of our mission. Kids. Escape. No time for sexy bikers. None. Nuh-uh. I would not let him into my happy place. That's what batteries were for.

I walked through the gap they opened in

the gates and wondered if I'd stepped into hell. I'd heard about the crap that went on inside places like this. Sarah and I used to watch motorcycle gang movies and joke about secret handshakes and clubhouses. The operative words being *used to*. Then she got involved with The Bastard. No more jokes after that.

"I'm Easy." The guy with the cropped hair and full sleeve of tattoos once again offered me his name and that aw-shucks grin.

"I'm still not."

He laughed—an honest chuckle and those freaking dimples winked at me. A biker with a sense of humor. And dimples. Who knew?

"This is Hardass and that's Gravedigger." Like Easy, Hardass was easy on the eyes. His hair was lighter, and he had a scruffy groove going on. Gravedigger was just freaking scary, but in a tall, dark, and sexy way. I'd bet my paycheck he didn't ever sleep alone. The club girls would line up around the block to take a walk on the wild side with him.

Easy didn't introduce me to the president. I didn't really want to know his name because my chances of getting out alive, in one piece, and with the kids were probably better by not knowing. Easy led the way, I followed, and the others brought up the rear—checking mine out the whole way. I resorted to a stupid taunt.

"Why don't y'all take a picture? It'll last longer."

Easy chuckled and slowed down until I stepped up beside him. "I'll make sure to get a good look once we get inside."

"Pig."

"Yes, ma'am, I am."

The dude winked at me and damn if my libido didn't start doing cartwheels. I reminded myself he was a killer. With a capital K. These people were not like the boys I'd grown up with. And they weren't like the guys I worked with. These people were criminals. I had no way of knowin' what kind of bad shit they were into, but I could guess from what little I knew about the Bastard and his Hell Dogs.

The spotlight snuffed out as soon as I stepped through the gate. Even though a few security lights were on, I couldn't tell much about the building. It was big. And built with what was probably granite or concrete. Maybe a warehouse or something. It sat on the outskirts of town and had a big-ass wall surrounding it. Not a fence. A wall made of concrete blocks and topped with concertina wire. Like a prison. Hell, with my luck, that's probably what this place had been in a former life. Talk about irony.

The guy with the president's patch pushed ahead of us and went through the door first. I stopped when he stopped, and the room went silent. "This is Samantha Prescott. She is my guest," he announced.

Without giving any of us a second glance, he walked across the room and disappeared through a door tucked in a little alcove along the back wall. As soon as the door closed, the sound cranked back up. I took my time looking around. A long, wooden bar stretched across the wall to my left, but I didn't think it was original to the building, even though it looked old. Just past the end closest to me, heavy, wooden double doors hid another room. I spotted an open door toward the other end of the bar and glimpsed what looked like a kitchen through it. In the main room, couches, chairs, tables, a pool table, big screen—scratch that—a giant screen TV, and about twenty guys occupied the space. I counted ten women, all sluts judging by their dress and their sexual activities with some of the bikers.

I took it all in with a glance and proceeded to ignore it. The architecture of this place blew me away. Soaring ceilings, marble floors, and a curving staircase to a balcony filled with arches. Now I really wanted to get a look at the outside. I couldn't decide which architectural school the place belonged to. It was a cross between Art Deco and Art Nouveau in style, not that any of these jerks would know the difference. This place had probably been a train station back in the day.

The ratty furniture, pool table, and giant screen seemed so incongruous in what had been the lobby. Then I noticed the dark splotch on the wall behind the pool table. What the hell was that? A pelt of some kind? It looked like silver-tipped black fur and there were massive paws and a head. Oh, holy hell. It was a wolf skin. Bolted to the wall. Literally. I didn't know whether to feel sorry for the dead wolf or get pissed that these idiots had defaced the wall by screwing spikes into it.

"You hungry?"

I glanced at Easy and I'm pretty sure my expression looked as skeptical as I felt.

"C'mon. I'll find you something to eat in the kitchen."

I couldn't help myself. I glanced down. If that wasn't a rolled-up sock in his pants, I was in serious trouble. When I looked up, he wore a darn good poker face, but his eyes twinkled. Still, I was curious—and hungry—so I followed him. Dang if that kitchen wasn't industrial strength. All stainless steel and a fridge that'd make Wolfgang Puck jealous. Two women sat at a long table in the back of the kitchen. They looked halfway normal, except for the leather vests and black Harley tee shirts they wore. I stiffened as I read the back of one—Property of Radar. My inner feminist got pissed off. The one facing the door looked up and blanched when she saw me. Easy saw her reaction too, and spoke to her.

"Sunny? You okay, hon?"

"Wow. You look just like Pretty Woman."

Pretty Woman? What the hell? I don't look anything like Julia Roberts. I started to say just that but she cut me off.

"You're her sister. Jonah and Noni's aunt." She looked me up and down again. "Twins?" She bounced out of her chair and trotted over. "I'm Sunny. I've been looking after the kids." Tears pooled in her eyes, surprising the heck outta me. "I'm really sorry for your loss. Russki called you Samantha, right?"

Russki must be the president and by his nickname, I'd guess his accent to be Russian now. I didn't want to think about him or any of these guys. This woman had just reminded me why I was here. I bit down on my lip to hold my own tears back. I took a couple of breaths to beat back my emotions. "Yeah. Sarah is—was my twin."

Metal clattered on metal, and I twisted my head to look at Easy. He'd dropped a big ol' cast iron fryin' pan on the massive commercial stove, but picked it back up as he said, "I wondered when I saw you."

I tried to laugh, but darn if the noise

coming out of my mouth didn't sound and feel more like a sob. "She was the oldest by about ten minutes. Momma said Sarah came into the world all soft and pretty while I had to fight my way out." I blinked a couple of times, and felt my face heat up. What in the heck possessed me to start jabbering like that? "I'm sorry. I don't know why I said that."

Easy tossed a huge slice of ham in the frying pan and snatched a carton of eggs from the fridge. He held it up and asked, "How do you like yours?"

"Doesn't matter. I'll eat just about anything."

His dimples came out to play, and he shifted as if his pants were too tight. I knew exactly what he was thinking, but he took the high road, even though those blue Husky eyes of his glittered with way too much cockiness. "Why don't you check out the..." He glanced down, and his expression turned sly. So much for the high road. Then he cleared his throat and continued, "...fridge for something to drink then go sit down. I'll bring your food over when it's done."

Sunny pulled me toward the table and the other woman. "Samantha—"

"Sam. Not even my momma called me by my full name."

She gave me a funny look with a tinge of pity hiding behind it, but then she smiled.

"This is Ginger. She belongs to Radar. And I'm Repo's old lady."

I saw a flash of diamond on her hand, along with a silver band on her finger. Wedding rings. Go figure. She pushed me down in an empty chair and asked what I wanted to drink. What I really wanted was a bottle of tequila, a salt shaker, and about a pound of limes. I asked for a Diet Coke.

"Do you mind drinking out of the can?"

Feeling a bit more like Alice in Wonderland than was comfortable, I tried to smile. "Can's fine."

The hair on the nape of my neck lifted, and I felt heat at my back. Easy. He leaned over my shoulder and slid a plate in front of me. I caught my breath at the scent of his cologne— no, not cologne, *him*. His scent filled my nose, and things low in my belly clenched. This guy was sex on a stick, and I wanted to eat him for breakfast like he was a deep-fried corn dog. Or would that be horn dog? Whoa! What was I thinking? Yeah, I still didn't have an answer for that because even as exhausted as I was, I'd do this dude in a heartbeat. He chuckled in my ear, and I couldn't breathe for a minute.

"Feeling's mutual, babe."

SEVEN

EASY

I WAS SO FUCKING PISSED. One day. Sam
had been here one gawddamn day and I was
ready to kill her. Right after I ripped the
heads off the two prospects sitting on the
merry-go-round looking beat all to hell. I'd get
right on that detail as soon as I reamed out
Sam Prescott. Ms. Hell on Wheels had
convinced the prospects to let her take the
kids to the playground. At least the men had
gone along as guards. Thank fuck one of the
prospects left on the gate was a Wolf. He
sounded the alarm, but not before all hell
broke loose in the park.

I toed the nearest body with my boot,
glancing toward the Russian. Noni was
wrapped around his thigh like a little
monkey. He stared at the three dead Hell
Dogs, ignoring the toddler peeking around his
leg.

Jonah shook loose of his aunt's grip and
came over. He spit on the nearest body. "It's
what they deserve."

Not hardly. These fuckers helped torture

and murder Pretty Woman. They deserved a much harder death than they got.

"The next one will die slow." Russki made that a promise.

"Fuckin' A." I dropped my hand to Jonah's shoulder, squeezed. The kid'd make a hellava Nightrider when he grew up, even if he wasn't a Wolf. Sam's face blanched as she watched the two kids. As tough as she acted, she still wasn't thrilled with the whole MC thing, especially where her sister's kids were concerned. Fuck that. She'd been spoutin' off about justice and an eye for an eye. Was all fuckin' gung ho until faced with the cold reality of dead bodies from our rival club. Digger, Hardy, and I would dump the remains at the nearest Hell Dogs' clubhouse, sending the message that the kids belonged to us now.

Sam gestured for Jonah to return to her side, and the kid obeyed. She was smart enough not to challenge the Russian over Noni. The little girl looked to be attached to his leg like some kid-sized burr.

I watched Sam, guessing at her thoughts. As soon as the opportunity presented itself, she'd snatch the kids and run. She wouldn't get far, but the idea unsettled my wolf. Me, too. I fought the attraction between us, fought the need to touch her.

If she was just some bitch, I'd fuck her and

move on. But she wasn't some random sweet butt. She was more, and my wolf had things all figured out. Thing was, Sam needed to fuckin' figure it out too. She was mine, and there wasn't a damn thing she could do about it. Course, she didn't know exactly what we were, either. She'd learn. Soon.

Most Wolves had some sense of fucking honor. We explain what we are to the women we claim as mates. I didn't give a good gawddamn. Sam was mine, and I'd make her fucking realize what she was to me before the night was over. First, though, we needed to take care of the scum.

A hand gripped my shoulder. A cold voice whispered an order in my ear. "Ease down, man."

Gravedigger. I inhaled, held my breath, let it out slow. I uncurled my fists, and my palms stung. My hands had partially shifted. The woman made me fuckin' lose control of my wolf. I wasn't some gawddamned beta. I didn't get lost in my hormones. And I damn sure didn't like where this bullshit was headed. I didn't want or need a mate. No matter how good Sam smelled, or how much my wolf wanted her.

Still speaking in muffled tones, Gravedigger added, "You should stay at the clubhouse."

"No. I gotta get away. Get her out of my

nose."

"Understood."

"Digger? She's gonna bolt."

He glanced over at the Russian, and I followed his gaze. Yeah, that wasn't gonna happen. Russki had her figured out too. He'd fucking handcuff her to a bed, a thought that made me growl. The Nightriders ran Nightshades, the biggest BDSM club in the Kansas City area. The Russian opened the place because he had certain proclivities. His eyes flicked to me, and his mouth twisted in a sardonic smile.

With what looked like a flick of his wrist, Noni now rode the Russian's hip, her arms around his neck. He gestured for the injured prospects to be taken back to the clubhouse. He followed, ushering Sam and Jonah in front of him. It was time for the rest of us to take out the trash.

By the time we got back from garbage detail, the kids were asleep, and Sam was locked in her room. My wolf didn't like it but it was probably smart on the Russian's part. If I saw her right then, I'd make a fool of myself. The brothers partied hard in the main room, and the sweet butts were all over them. A couple of the girls looked my way when I came in, and one came over carrying a beer, opening a couple more buttons on her shirt as she walked.

I dropped into a chair and she draped herself on my lap. I took the beer but dumped her on the floor. She looked surprised for a minute then smiled as she settled between my knees.

"Ooh. I know what you want, sweetie." She worked the buckle on my belt. My wolf snapped at her. Fuck. I didn't want to get it on with this chick. Sam really was my mate. Digger noticed my pathetic lack of enthusiasm and laughed.

He walked over, stopped in front of me, whipped out his dick, and grabbed the bitch by the hair, jerking her around. "You want a real man, babe. Suck this." He forced her mouth open and rammed in.

I saluted him with my beer, rolled out of the chair, and headed outside. I wasn't fit for company if I'd turn down a blow job from a sweet butt.

🐾 🐾 🐾 🐾

MOST OF THE BROTHERS were still sleeping off their hangovers. Those not sawing logs were on guard duty or working. Besides Nightshades, we had a strip club called Chasin' Tail, Ryder Bail Bonds, and a few other enterprises that weren't strictly on the books. At the moment, only the cadre and Sam were in the clubroom.

"Look, buster."

Sam hammered her index finger into the

Russian's chest and I froze. Digger hadn't pulled his knife so she wasn't dead. Yet.

"No, *devushka*, you will look. Jonah and Noni are under the protection of the Nightriders. Under *my* protection. They stay here. You wish to leave, go. You will not be leaving with them."

"You're as big a bastard as Noni's father."

She balled up her hand and swung before I could move. The Russian caught her fist, spun her around, and had her wrapped up with her back to his chest before she could blink. My wolf whined, and I all but swatted his muzzle to keep him buried inside me. Damn thing didn't want the Russian touching her. I wasn't too thrilled about the situation myself, but my momma didn't raise no stupid children. Telling the Russian to get his hands off her would get me dead right quick. When her struggles ramped up, the Russian bent his head to whisper into her ear, the words just loud enough for Hardy, Digger, and me to hear.

"The man who would claim Noni is my enemy. She is under my personal protection. I will kill anyone—*anyone*—who tries to take her. Do you understand, Samantha Prescott?"

I didn't want to laugh. Damn if she didn't look like a little kitten all spit-n-hissy with her claws out and about as effective. This was about discipline, not sex. Russki was my

Alpha, and when I reminded my wolf of that, he snarled but relaxed a little.

"You are here because you are the only living relative of the *deti*, of the children."

She sputtered and tried to kick his shin, but he simply tossed her on the nearest couch. Luckily, she was smart enough to stay there.

"This is the truth, Samantha Prescott, so hear it and understand. What you want means nothing to me. Jonah and Noni belong to the Nightriders now. We will keep them safe from those who wish them harm. You saw what happened last night. Had they been taken, or hurt, you would have been responsible. You cannot take care of them, keep them safe. We can and we will. They remain here."

She opened her mouth to argue, but she recognized something in the Russian's expression and remained silent. I breathed a little easier. Sam wasn't out of the woods yet. My wolf and my dick both sweated that fact. I wanted this woman like I'd never wanted another. I didn't sleep because my fucking balls weren't only blue, they ached and burned like some bitch had smashed them with a hot iron. And that bitch was Sam Prescott. My wolf recognized her before I did, that first night when she arrived at the gate. We both wanted her but until she figured out how to play nice with us, I wasn't about to let the wolf loose. The Russian would snap Sam's neck in a heartbeat if she didn't get with the program.

Sam still reminded me of that pissed-off kitten, but I could almost see the wheels turning in her head. I might want to fuck her until we were both blind, but I was a realist. She'd snatch the kids and cut and run at the first opportunity. What she wasn't smart enough to figure out is that she'd be dead within twenty-four hours. There were about forty of us here in the south Kansas City area, but the Nightriders had chapters in all fifty states. The Russian was our national President. If he snapped his fingers, over a thousand Nightriders would be here within hours, lining up to do whatever the hell he ordered. Not all of us were Wolves, but even the brothers who were strictly human would spill blood for the patch. Problem was, there were almost as many Hell Dogs. And they were huntin' her.

"I am not in the habit of explaining my actions, but I will make an exception this one time." Russki stared down at Sam until she blinked and gulped. She finally nodded to indicate she'd listen. "I have been checking on your sister and her life before Easy stumbled into it." An expression of sadness mixed with disgust crossed his face. "Your sister was a bad judge of men. We have located the man who was her husband, the man who donated his sperm to create Jonah." He watched until she acknowledged this information with another nod. "He will be dead by sunset tomorrow."

We'd managed to get Jonah to open up a little. He told us his old man was a cop and that the son of a bitch beat on Sarah. The one time Jonah tried to stop him, he'd put the kid in the hospital. They'd run away, and his mom had ended up with the Bastard because he promised to keep the fuckwad cop away. Then she came up pregnant with Noni and things went bad. Even without names, having that much info meant we could track down the asshole.

Russki's eyes flicked to Digger. The SOB might be a cop, but he was dirty. Both of the men who'd sired those kids were the swamp scum of humanity and no great loss to the Universe. Seeing them dead would be no skin off my nose, but I hoped Gravedigger made the cop's death look like an accident. Less bullshit that way.

Sam stared at the Russian, her mouth hangin' open, and I recognized the flash of fear in her expression. My wolf stirred inside me. I wanted to go to her, wrap my arms around her, and tell her things would be okay. I'd be lyin' so I didn't. But the feeling was there just the same. The damn woman kept stirring up all sorts of emotions in me. And my senses were on overload, not to mention my dick was so hard I figured it would break if I had to bend over.

The Russian glanced at me. We'd picked up some rumors about Noni's father. The sick sonavabitch wanted to sell Noni to the highest bidder after he had his sick thrills with her. Wolves like us weren't angels, but gawddamn, you didn't fuckin' do shit like that. Every fuckin' one of us had a soft spot when it came to kids. Wolves don't procreate well. When we're lucky enough to find a mate, they miscarry more often than not. Probably nature's way of keeping our numbers stable, but damn. It hurt. Hurt our women. Hurt us. Children were gifts. My dick twitched, reminding me that it was really interested in making babies with Sam. I took a quick step backwards. What the fuck was I thinking?

Sam sat up straight, but didn't push off the couch. Her eyes flashed and her chin jutted up. "Jonah's father is a cop. You can't do anything to him."

"We can and we will." Russki's mouth twisted in a display of nonchalance. It wouldn't be the first cop we'd taken out. "But this is none of your concern."

"Excuse me? It damn sure is! Sarah was my sister and Jonah is my nephew. Noni is my niece. Anything that involves them or happens to them is my concern. I'm their legal guardian."

"And I am their protector." The Russian glowered at Sam, and I wanted to tell her to shut the fuck up before she totally pissed him off. People who pissed him off did so at their own risk. "As for the man you and Jonah call the Bastard, he will also be dealt with, but for reasons far more personal than being Noni's sperm donor."

We all watched her, waiting for her reaction, and I could see her thinking. Fuck. She already knew why that SOB wanted Noni. I saw it in her eyes. That's why she'd come armed, probably figuring we ran with the Dogs. Like that would ever fucking happen. Her nose wrinkled up and I had this insane need to kiss her until she relaxed, starting with her nose and ending up somewhere in the vicinity of her pussy. Man, I was in so much trouble. At the rate she was pushing, she'd be lucky to live out the day, and the way my wolf was pacing, he'd make me do something stupid like fight for her. I wanted to shift and go hunting, bring down a deer and drink the fresh blood. Maybe that would keep him in line because I damn sure didn't like the way he was acting.

Sam finally nodded, as if she'd come to some sort of decision. "Okay. I'll admit those

SOBs are sorry excuses for men. Y'all taking...*care* of them saves me the trouble." She leaned forward and braced her elbows on her thighs. "And until they're out of the picture, the kids probably are safer here."

The Russian started to speak, but she held up a finger cutting him off. "Personally, I think they'd be safer at my place in Utah because the Hell Dogs don't know about me."

Laughter erupted in the room. From all of us. I rolled my eyes. "Babe, I got news for you. The Hell Dogs know all about you. The word is already out on the street that you're here to get the kids. Why the hell do you think they hit you in the park yesterday?" Cold seeped into my blood at the thought of the Dogs getting their hands on her, of any man touching her. "The Russian's right, babe. You and the kids need to stay here where we can protect you." *Where I can fuck you nine ways from Sunday.*

"Listen to Easy, Samantha Prescott. You will stay here with us, and you will not argue about this."

As fast as a cat, she pushed off the couch and stalked to the Russian, standing toe to toe with him. "My turn. You hear this, you sorry son of a bitch. I will not be one of your club whores."

I couldn't see the Russian's face, and I wasn't sure I wanted to. I glanced over at

Digger. He could see what both sides in this standoff were doing. When I caught his eye, he lifted a shoulder, but his expression didn't change. I couldn't figure out if that meant he'd be going to work on Sam or what. My wolf whined. Damn straight Sam wouldn't be a club whore. She was mine. I'd fucking rip out the throat of any man who tried to touch her. Except for the Russian. *Mother. Stupid children*, I reminded my wolf.

Quick as a snake, the Russian struck. His hand wrapped around her neck, jerked her closer, and then he kissed her. Hard. After he turned her loose, she spit on the floor and swiped the back of her hand across her mouth.

Fuck. She was dead. My dick was not a happy cowboy, and my wolf was pissed off. My dick had figured to get inside her at some point in the immediate future. Me and the wolf had every intention of claiming Sam as our mate, and he wanted to bite the Russian—even if Russki was the Alpha—for kissing Sam. Digger was suddenly standing next to me. I didn't realize I'd stepped closer to the Russian or that my hands were curled into fists until I discovered I'd shifted them into claws. That's twice I lost control. I breathed through panicked rage, and my hands went back to human. Digger gave me a WTF look. Yeah, I knew that feeling. I couldn't be fucking moonstruck. But I was. When my heart stopped pounding so loud in my ears that I could hear again, I tuned into what the boss was saying.

"You will go back to Utah. Get the things you must have. Leave the rest. You will live here with the *deti*."

"I told you—"

This time he wrapped his hand around her throat cutting off the next word. "You tell me nothing, and do as I say." The Russian turned his head, fixed his gaze on me. "Easy."

I froze. Did he realize what my wolf had tried to do? I damn sure hoped my voice didn't crack when I answered. "Yeah?"

"Take the Hummer and this one who is not a club whore. Get her things and come back here. Do you understand?"

Fuck. I'd just been sentenced to a road trip through hell.

EIGHT

EASY

WE LEFT THE CLUBHOUSE that afternoon about three after Sam explained to the kids that I was taking her to Utah to pack up her stuff because she was moving to Mission Springs. Jonah seemed upset but settled when he realized she wasn't taking the Jeep. I guess he worried she'd take off and not come back. The Russian held Noni during the goodbyes, and the little dickens had to be coerced to give Sam a gooey, Nilla Wafer flavored bye-bye kiss.

We stopped in Hays, Kansas for gas and truck-stop food about seven. Sam didn't like me waiting outside the door of the ladies room for her. She accused me of not trusting her. My response was, "Yeah, and?"

"Where would I go? You have the keys."

My dick and my wolf might want to play house, but my brain wasn't complete mush yet. The woman was slick. She could con an east-bound trucker into taking her back to the clubhouse, and she'd figure out some way to snatch the kids. That'd be signing her death warrant, and that flat-out wasn't happening.

There ain't much to look at on I-70 in that part of Kansas. It was dark when we crossed into Colorado, so there wasn't even the hint of mountains on the horizon to break up the flatlands. When she crossed her legs and looked stubborn, I pulled into another truck stop on the north side of Denver just after midnight. I could do with a cup of coffee and some rare meat myself. After she did her thing, we settled into a booth in the attached restaurant.

I sat across from her, which pissed off my wolf. He wanted me to touch her, be close to her, and he kept pacing just beneath my skin keeping me off balance and snarly. We ordered, and Sam went back to ignoring me. I got a little pissed too. She managed to look everywhere but at me. I'm no prize, but I've never had to fight to get between a girl's legs either.

I glanced around the place, noting every other female there. Our waitress was young and perky in all the right places. She gave me a little wink and a big flirty smile every time she refilled my coffee cup. I tracked the girl through the room with my eyes and considered.

We'd made good time so far. Taking a short break wouldn't put a dent in the schedule.

Maybe I could handcuff Sam in the Hummer while I gave the waitress a ride on her break. I sort of liked the idea, but my wolf wasn't having any of it. Sumbitch decided it was Sam or no one, just like back at the clubhouse. Fuck. Which was the whole idea my dick tried to remind the animal side of me.

Sam moved, and I glanced at her out of the corner of my eye. She was smoothing her forearms with the palms of her hands, and then she looked up at me. Her gaze knocked the air out of my lungs. Angry. Scared. And turned on. I inhaled. Oh yeah. She was definitely all three of those. I ignored the stink of burnt toast and ammonia to concentrate on the underlying scent. Honeysuckle and gunpowder. Weirdest damn arousal scent I'd ever sniffed, but fuck if it didn't turn me on. My dick was ready to rip the buttons off my fly.

"Ow. What the fuck?" Sam had nailed my shin with the toe of her boot. Her expression remained poker-faced, until I looked closely at her eyes. They'd narrowed and damn if there wasn't some blue fire sparking in their depths. "What was that for?"

"General principles." She shimmied to the edge of the booth and stood up. "I have to pee again. You pay."

"I'm not done."

"Oh yeah, you are."

A new scent wafted in, and it wasn't bacon. I stood up so I could get closer. Vinegar? What the hell? Was she jealous? I tossed a couple of crumpled twenties on the table and followed Sam out, totally intrigued now. My wolf was all happy dancing.

Sam didn't like me looking at other women.

I followed her to the ladies room, and after she entered, ducked into the men's to take care of my own business. I was waiting for her when she emerged, still all pissy. She glowered at me and headed toward the convenience store part of the truck stop. Filling the biggest cup they had with Diet Coke, she arched a brow until I dug out the money to pay for it. I grabbed a couple bottles of water, followed her to the checkout, paid, and escorted her to the Hummer.

Staring out the windshield, I pointed the Hummer north toward Cheyenne. We'd follow the Rockies Front Range up I-25 until it was time to head west again on I-80. Sam stared out her window, pointedly ignoring me. That was fine. My wolf was enjoying all the conflicting scents she gave off. My dick was a happy camper too. She wanted us. And fuck if we weren't going to get in her pants before this trip was over. Maybe this wasn't the road trip from hell after all.

🐾 🐾 🐾 🐾

BESIDES CHECKING THE CLOCK, the only way I knew dawn was coming was the faint graying of the clouds in my rear view mirror. We made damn good time, despite some heavy rain between Cheyenne and Rock Springs. The Great Basin area was almost as flat as eastern Colorado. Sam sat scrunched up against the door of the Hummer. She'd been awake about an hour. I could tell by the way her breathing changed, though she kept her face turned away from me.

I focused on the asphalt interstate winding through the Utah mountains. We'd left the rain behind, but I expected snow to start falling any minute now that we were making the climb toward Salt Lake. Sam hadn't said a word since a stop in Rawlins, and, as she'd been asleep, I left things quiet. Problem was, I hated silence. Always had. Reaching for the radio, I punched the button for the CD. Duran Duran filled the air.

"Turn it off." Sam's voice sounded like she'd been chewing rocks.

"It speaks."

"Shut up."

"Make me."

"What? Are you like...six?"

"I'm not the one acting like a spoiled brat."

"You don't know a damn thing about me."

I turned down the sound. "Then tell me about you."

"You loved her."

"Who?"

"Sarah."

I had to think a minute. I didn't know Sarah's name until after her murder and Sam showed up to claim the kids. She was Pretty Woman in my head, not *Sarah*. "Why would you say that?"

More silence. She shifted in the seat, and I glanced at her. Were those tears she blinked away? Shit. Tears totally sucked and messed up every man I knew. Including me. Aw hell, especially me.

"Everybody did."

"Did what?"

"Loved Sarah."

"Seems more like she loved the wrong people. And just FYI? I didn't love her. Didn't know her that well. She saved my life. I owed her. That's all." No need to mention I'd wanted to fuck her. Hell, I pretty much wanted to fuck every woman, but some still-functioning part of my brain warned me it would be a mistake to mention that to Sam. Then again, after meeting Sam, I knew which twin I'd pick so previous thoughts didn't count.

"Maybe so, but everyone still loved her. She was...soft. Sweet. Nice."

I considered my first impressions of both women. Honeysuckle and sweet tea versus steel magnolia. I wasn't any sort of psychologist but I got the sense Sam felt like she was somehow less lovable than her twin. Not by me, that was for damn sure.

"Hasn't anyone ever loved you, babe?"

Her left shoulder rolled up into a little hunch and she wouldn't look at me. "Sure."

"Well, for your information, I like my women to be something more than soft, sweet, and nice." I glanced at her. She was listening even if she wasn't looking at me. "Hell on wheels. Steel magnolia." I grinned. "Honeysuckle and gunpowder."

She huffed out a breath and ruffled her bangs. "What does that even mean?"

"You, babe. I like my women just like you."

Folding her arms across her chest, Sam tucked her feet up into the seat and went back to staring out the window. Everything was gray, and the first snowflakes splattered against the windshield. Occasional headlights glowed on the eastbound side of the highway, but we might as well have been driving through an endless gray tunnel. Sam was quiet for so long I figured she'd gone back to sleep so her question caught me by surprise.

"What's going happen to me and the kids?" Her voice was flat, unemotional, but she was tight, like she was all wound up inside.

"You're under the Russian's protection. You'll be safe."

"From you?"

Was that interest in her voice? "Babe, you'll never be safe from me."

Sam was mine. I'm not sure exactly when I figured it out. Maybe it was when I saw her standing there outside the gate stinking of ammonia and pepper sauce. Fear and determination. She couldn't fight what we were, what we would be—mates. Me? I was going to fuck her comin' and goin', and I was going to do it damn soon before my dick broke off. I'd been hard since the first moment I saw her.

"What the hell am I going to do?"

She sounded defeated. I glanced over again, but she was staring out the side window, and I only caught a glimpse of her profile. "Whatever it takes, Sam." I reached over and stroked her thigh. I had to touch her, but cringed when the muscles under her jeans jumped under my hand. She was skittish, scared. I guess she had every right to be given the circumstances. But she hadn't figured out the one truth between us. I wouldn't hurt her. I couldn't. She was mine. I wanted to mark her, roll her in my scent so every Wolf in the gawddamned country knew she was my mate. Moonstruck. That's our word for what was happening. The mating heat was coming, and it would hit me hard. I'd be a snarly beast until I claimed her. Until she admitted she belonged to me. Fuck. She didn't even know what I was.

To Sam, I'd be the Big Bad Wolf. Most humans freaked when they found out about us. The human Nightriders didn't know that some of us could shift into wolves. And it's not like we could bite them to give them the *lupi* DNA. Hell, a mated couple could have a dozen kids if they were lucky, and only one child might carry the dominant gene. If the fetus survived. Odds were stacked against us. Losing babies ripped us apart—everyone in the pack. When a Wolf mated, his woman became the pack's to protect.

I had to touch her so I shifted in my seat. The move let my hand brush against her thigh again. When she sat still, I left my fingers there. My wolf settled immediately. He was a patient hunter. I needed to follow his lead. I reminded my dick of that.

Taking a chance, I stroked one finger along Sam's thigh. She shivered but in a good way. Progress. I continued to pet her, and a few minutes later, she surprised me with a little snorting snore. She'd dozed off. She had to be exhausted. I know she didn't get but a couple hours of sleep at the clubhouse. I could hear her breathing and moving in the room next to mine. She'd been going for forty-eight hours with very little sleep in the middle.

She slept through the mountains. I kept

my hand on her thigh, the heat of her searing my palm. I wanted to avoid Salt Lake City, but this was snow season, and the "Pass Closed" warning signs were up. I didn't have a choice. We had real snow now, but the Hummer ate that shit for breakfast.

When we hit the edge of Brighton, I squeezed her thigh. Sam dragged her fingers through her hair, and it stood up in tired spikes. The skin around her eyes still looked bruised, and she wouldn't meet my gaze straight on. She mumbled something about killing for some caffeine so I looked for a place. She pointed out a little store up ahead and promised they made good coffee.

I drank mine standing up out in the parking lot. Sam was huddled in her goosedown jacket. I wore my leather. The local Barney Fife drove by slow and gave me the once over. I saluted him with my coffee cup and a raised middle finger. The nearest brothers were in Layton, which was about halfway between Salt Lake City and Ogden. They'd come bail my ass out if I got busted.

"Wow, you really know how to win friends and make enemies."

"Yup. It's a gift."

Sam rolled her eyes as she set her coffee cup on the hood of the Hummer. Placing her hands on the back of her neck, Sam arched her back until her perky little tits were visible even under that thick coat she wore. My dick did the downward dog, sat up, and fucking begged. I even whimpered. I swear she knew what she was doing to me. She raised her hands above her head, twisted left then right, and bent over. Her sweet ass was just begging for me to rip her jeans over the curve and sink into her sweet pussy. That was the plan and both my wolf and my dick were on board.

"Easy?" She watched me from between her knees. Damn but she was flexible.

I wanted to check my chin for drool, but I'd have to surrender my man card if I found some. "Yeah?"

She straightened up and glanced at me over her shoulder. "You coming?"

NINE

SAM

MY LIBIDO OBVIOUSLY wasn't paying attention to my common sense. Dang. Where the hell had that line come from? I mean seriously, could I open my mouth and spit out a more explicit innuendo? Which made me want to laugh because I'd bet my very expensive carbon snow skis Easy was so not my type. I wanted to stick my fingers in my ears and sing "La la la la" until my libido found an earworm to listen to—preferably a song not sung by some sexy-voiced rock star— so that hussy would stop whispering sexy ideas in my ear.

I laughed at the expression on the dude's face. I couldn't help myself. His impressive erection was a millimeter away from popping all the buttons on his fly, and sweat beaded up on his forehead. Oh, yeah. Easy lived up to his name. Problem was, I felt more than a little squirmy in my pants, too. Why did this guy turn me on? He was rough. Crude. Should have the words "bad boy" all in caps tattooed on his forehead. And I hoped he closed his gaping mouth long enough to put me up against the Hummer and fuck me until I couldn't breathe.

Just the thought had my thighs tensing and pressing together. I wasn't a one-night-stand sort of girl, but for Easy? I might just make an exception. He was bad news of the worst sort. He'd love me and leave me without a backward glance, and that so wasn't going to work. No telling how long I'd be stuck with the Nightriders. The guy they called the Russian was not a man you said no to. Well, maybe once. Then your family would be lucky if your body was ever found.

Licking my lips because my mouth had gone dry, I glanced up. I was in so much trouble now. And damn if my libido didn't have the freaking pompoms out doing cheers.

EASY

HOLY FUCK. The bitch knew exactly what she was doing to me. And she was laughing. At. Me. Pissed me right the hell off. Any other female, I'd have had her legs spread within five minutes of walking her inside the clubhouse. Or on her knees sucking me off. My wolf brushed up against my insides and whined happily. He liked that idea. So did I. If the cops hadn't already driven by once, I'd just rip her jeans off and put her up against the Hummer. Fuck her right here. I shouldn't care.

But I did. And that's why I hadn't taken her at the clubhouse. Or on the trip. Or standing right here. Dammit, didn't she know I was trying to be a...fuck. What was I trying to be? Not myself, that's for damn sure. Well enough of that shit.

She stopped laughing, and her eyes were glued to my hard on. When she looked up and licked her lips, that was it. Any control I might have had snapped.

"Get in the fucking Hummer."

She stared at me, eyes narrowing and fists clenching at her sides. "Excuse me? What did you just say?"

I pushed up against her, backing her against the driver's door. "You heard me. You have about five minutes to get me where we're going, get inside, and get fuckin' naked."

She arched a brow like she was one of those society bitches. "What if I say no?"

I leaned in, sniffed her right behind the ear. Not that I needed to. If I reached down and grabbed her crotch, she'd be wet. The ripe scent of her lust—a richer, lusher version of her normal scent—filled my lungs. Honeysuckle and gunpowder. I grabbed her hand and pressed it against my dick. "I'm fuckin' tired of blue balls, babe. Get in the gawddamned Hummer before I strip you right here. I don't give a fuck if we both end up in jail for indecent exposure and lewd acts. My dick is gonna be inside your pussy in five minutes or else."

Thank God she took me seriously. She climbed through my door and bounced across the console to the passenger seat. She was panting, her nostrils flared as she stared at me. "Start driving."

"Yes, ma'am." Finally! We were finally on the same fucking page of this program.

She gave short, terse directions, and I slammed on the brakes, sending gravel flying as I stopped in front of one of those A-frame ski chalet cabin places. She was out and headed toward the door while I was still slamming the transmission into Park. I had enough sense to grab the keys and lock the Hummer before I caught up to her at the door. I grabbed her, lifted her feet off the decking, and braced her against the wall. Her long, muscular legs wrapped around my waist as her arms hugged my neck.

"Too late. It's been six minutes." I kicked in the door.

"Upstairs," she panted, slamming the door behind us.

I found the stairs and all but ran up them. "Left."

Another door, another kick. A bed.

When I tumbled her to the mattress, she

kept her legs and arms hooked around me. As I followed her down, she twisted, using the momentum to roll on top of me. I could deal with this just as long as she got my fucking dick inside her now. Mouth. Pussy. I wasn't choosy.

"It's going to be fast," she warned me.

"I can live with that."

Sam pushed the cut off my shoulders with one hand and tugged on my tee shirt with the other. I sat up, jerked both of them off and peeled her shirt over her head. Sam used both hands to push me back down on the bed. As soon as my head hit the pillow, she ran her hands in one hard sweep over my chest then lowered her head to scrape teeth over my flesh. My dick throbbed in time to each nibble she took.

I cupped her tits in my hands, raised up to suck her nipple after teasing it with my tongue. I tweaked her other nipple between my thumb and forefinger, twisting and pulling. She gasped, lifted her head, and stared at me. Her eyes had gone darker, from sky to ocean. She wanted this fast? I was ready. Flipping her, I dragged her jeans off, but had forgotten about her boots. She sat up to help while I stripped out of my own. Then I just stood there. Looking. She was so fucking beautiful. I muttered that thought out loud, then repeated it louder.

"Fucking beautiful." I dropped to my knees, spread her thighs. Her pink folds were slick, plump. Waiting for my mouth. The taste of her burst on my tongue. Sweet. Smoky. Like her scent. While I nipped and sucked on her clit, I slipped my thumb into her. Greedy muscles tugged against my invasion, wanting me deeper. I pushed a finger in, then two. She rode my hand, bucking as I used my teeth on her. Her muscles clenched around me, and I pumped harder, faster, felt her inner muscles flutter, and then she gasped. Her muscles locked, and she hung there, suspended, for what felt like minutes. When she fell, her muscles turned liquid, her eyes deeper than the midnight sky.

"Damn, baby." My voice was husky, my throat dry. Her skin flushed as heat drenched her. It pumped from her, fueled my need, pulsing through my whole system like a hit of adrenaline. I was fucking greedy now. I wanted all of her. I dragged her back on the mattress, climbed on beside her, and spread her legs wider.

I teased her folds with the head of my dick just long enough to get it slick, and then I plunged into her. She screamed as her inner muscles stretched.

"Too much. Too much." She beat on my back with her fists, and I captured her protests in my mouth, kissing her hard and deep, a wet kiss meant to imprint her on my soul with a promise of leaving a bit of me clinging in her heart.

Mine. My brain screamed it, and my wolf howled. Fuck. There was no doubt. As soon as my dick sank in all the way, when my balls teased the sweet curve of her ass, I knew. She was mine. Moonstruck. I'd fucking found my mate, and she had no clue what the hell I was. I wasn't human. Not entirely. *Lupi versi pellis.* Literally translated, it meant the man who wears the skin of a wolf. Wolf shifter. And everyone knows Wolves mate for life.

It was too late to turn back, to stop what was happening between us. I wore her scent on my skin, her taste already a part of me, a living, breathing thing inside me. Stunned, I lay there, braced on my hands.

She arched up, her mouth seeking my mouth. Her lips fused on mine, her tongue pushed in, slicked along the side of mine. Greedy, she fed on my lips. The kiss spiked her temperature. Her need. I pushed her away, back against the pillows. I wanted her. All of her. And I would take what I wanted. I bent to kiss her again. I left her lips slick and wet, and my dick throbbed. It fucking loved her pussy, but it wanted to slide into her sweet mouth, too. I dragged teeth over her jawline, her collar bone. Found her tit. I nipped and then kissed to soothe the bite of pain. Her heart hammered under my mouth. Her muscles tensed again as my hips dragged away from her and then surged deep.

"Too slow," she complained and twisting hard, she flipped our positions. Her impatient hands pressed my shoulders against the bed as her knees squeezed my flanks and ribs. She tugged my nipples, and her eyes glittered. "Two can play that game."

I groaned and she laughed. Rising on her knees, my dick slid out of her. I grabbed her hips to force her back down, but she beat me to it. Laughter, sharp and bright, changed, became a growl of pure pleasure locked in her throat as she rose and fell again. She clenched around me, drove me mad with her teasing. Rearing up, I clamped my mouth on her tit, sucking her in until I felt her heart beat against my tongue. This. Her. She was the flavor, the heat, the scent of mate. She arched, letting me fill her. I dropped my hands to her hips, held her as I drove up into her depths. She met me, thrust for thrust, until she drove me back against the bed. Bracing her hands on either side of my head, she rocked her hips and pistoned off her knees, setting a furious pace.

The dark, dangerous edge of need sliced through me. Sam's face glowed with life, alive with pleasure and intent on driving us both crazy. She rode me as if our lives depended on it. In ways she didn't understand, my life did.

I didn't believe my dick could get any harder, but it did, and it throbbed in time to her heartbeat, to my heartbeat. Heat enveloped us, the air almost too thick to breathe, and my vision dimmed. Sam was a blur of blonde and blue as I fell into her gaze.

"So close," she cried. "Come with me, Easy. Let go." She screamed as the first shudders of her orgasm locked her muscles. She screamed and screamed, until her voice was raw.

I flipped us, my body plunging into hers. The air looked as if it had turned red as light blurred around us. My seed pumped into her, and I raised my head adding my voice to that of the wolf howling his joy. Our joy. Sam's and mine.

TEN

SAM

CRUD. Crud-crud-crud crap-on-a-cracker. What the hell was I thinking? Oh, wait. I wasn't. My libido had hijacked my brain despite the near constant litany of my inability to think rationally when it came to Easy. I wanted to move. I really did. But my bones had melted, and my muscles felt like oatmeal. I was draped over Easy's chest, and he wasn't helping any. His arms anchored me in place.

This was such a huge mistake. But dang the man could kiss. And his cock. I was totally in love with his cock. It stirred beneath me, pressing against my stomach. My thighs clenched. Holy hell, I could *not* still be horny. I ordered my body to move, to lift off Easy and roll away. Nothing happened except my cheek brushing against his chest. I wanted to bury my nose against his throat and simply breathe him in. I could still taste him on my tongue—something spicy, but deep and rich, like mincemeat, or a Fig Newton. Only with tequila. Yeah. Kissing Easy was like doing tequila shots followed by cookies. I was in so freaking much trouble.

I didn't do bad boys. Ever. Watching Sarah's fatal attractions convinced me early on I wanted none of that. In fact, I didn't date much. Guys made great friends, especially given I worked ski patrol and search and rescue at the mountain resorts. Getting tangled up just didn't make sense. Neither did laying here naked, horny, and ready for round two with the sexy biker I was currently using as a mattress.

Fighting the urge to rub my entire body against his sweat-slicked skin, I tumbled into the fantasy of licking him. All over. His cock twitched again. I swore the man gave off sex pheromones.

Easy stirred beneath me, and I bounced as he took a deep breath. "You think too hard, Sam. Go to sleep."

"I can't."

His cock throbbed this time and grew longer and harder. Oh shit. I was gonna get my wish. "In that case."

Less than a heartbeat later, he was on top of me, his hips settled between my legs like he belonged there. And dang if I didn't think the same thing. No man had ever...fit me the way this one did. He was a stranger, but he knew me intimately. I pushed against his shoulders as the head of his cock pressed against my entrance. He stopped immediately. Raised his head. Stared down at me, those Siberian husky eyes of his shining like blue fire.

"I don't even know your name," I murmured.

He hovered there, holding both of us on the brink of something wonderful, something...magical.

"Easy."

I shook my head. "No. That's not who you are."

A slow, wicked smile curled his lips. "Yeah, it is."

I didn't want to beg, but I would if I had to. "Please? It's important to me."

He blinked and an expression I couldn't decipher, much less explain, flitted across his face.

"Elijah. Elijah Cross."

Elijah. The name filled my heart. Old fashioned. Powerful. Untamed. Yes. *This* is who he was.

"Hello, Elijah Cross. Make love to me."

His dimples came out to play as his cock plunged into me. I gasped in surprise, and then my whole body turned liquid with need.

"Yes, ma'am."

He didn't speak again. Neither did I. I had no words, or breath to push them out of my brain had I been able to form them. He rocked into me, going so deep I felt his balls kiss me. I arched up to meet him, stroke for stroke, and when he dipped his head to take my nipple into his mouth, I thought I would shatter.

"No," he mumbled around my breast. "Not yet." He slowed our rhythm, stopped. I sunk my nails into the firm muscles of his butt, but he only laughed. "I like your claws, woman. Use them."

Easy raised his head and offered a wolfish grin. My libido did fist pumps while my brain screamed, *"Stranger danger! RUN!"*

Then he tongued my other breast, and I told my brain to shut the hell up. This man was seeping into my skin. I was in soooo much trouble, but I couldn't make myself care. He was a stranger. Being stuck in a vehicle with him for twenty hours, having hot monkey sex with him, and now having him seduce me with slow kisses and a penchant for my clawing his ass did not make us lovers. Or friends. It certainly didn't make us anything more, despite the hope my heart whispered.

Mine. I wanted this man. Wanted him on a deep, visceral level I couldn't comprehend given the circumstances.

Mine.

Wait. What? That thought didn't belong to me. I pushed at his shoulders again. "Easy.

Stop."

He did. Just like that. His cock throbbed once deep inside me and then even it stilled. How the heck could he do that? Easy stared at me, his expression calm, but blue fire flickered in the depths of his eyes again.

"Did you say something?"

A slow blink and when I saw his eyes again, that spark in them was even brighter. "No."

Damn. I never ever wanted to play poker with this man. He leaned on one elbow, and with his other hand, he flicked my bangs off my forehead.

"We done talking now?"

I laughed. I couldn't help myself. He was such a typical guy. "And if we are?"

"Just askin', babe. If we're done, then I can get on with fuckin' your brains out."

Oh. Yeah. I could get with that program, but that unheard voice still bugged me. "Are you sure you didn't say something?"

"Fuck, babe. What did you hear? I'll say whatever you want just so we can start fucking again."

"I—" His cock throbbed and I lost all ability to think. "Never mind."

EASY
I WAS IN SO MUCH fucking trouble. This woman was driving me crazy. My wolf wanted

to come out to play, rolling in the sheets where Sam and I had just fucked. He wanted to lick her from her lips to her toes and oh yeah, he wanted to spend time with his nose in her pussy, and he was more than happy that I had plans to do exactly that. God she smelled good and tasted better. I wanted to suck her pussy until she screamed. I wanted to pound my dick in her cunt until she had no room for any other man. Just me. Sam was mine, and I'd fucking kill any man who touched her.

You know that little part of the brain that clobbers a guy with a clue-by-four and says, "This is a really bad idea, asshole?" Yeah, I told that fucker to shut the hell up. Sam was ours, the wolf's and mine. She'd just fucking have to accept that I was a Wolf. And a Nightrider. That same part of my brain wondered which one would upset her the most. I stuck some duct tape over my brain's mouth. I was gonna claim her as my mate and put my property patch on her ASAP.

Slipping out of her, I kissed my way down to her navel. Sam grabbed the hair on the top of my head to get my attention.

"Didn't you say something about fucking?"

Swiping my tongue through the curls on her pubes, I propped my chin on her mound and pretended to think. "I can fuck you with more than just my dick, baby."

Her eyes glittered and her breath hitched. I felt deep muscles flutter under my chin. Oh, yeah. My woman loved it when I ate her out. I caught her thighs and pushed them over my shoulders and braced one hand under her sweet ass. My dick was gonna get up close and personal with that particular sweetness sooner than later, but right now, I was hungry.

I tongue fucked her and used a finger to rub and tease her clit. Then I switched, using my tongue and teeth on her clit while I finger fucked her. She was so damn wet I spread her juices all the way down her ass crack. My thumb couldn't resist the temptation. I pressed against her asshole, but didn't enter when she tensed up. I liked sex rough and hard, but there was no way in hell I'd ever hurt Sam or force her to do something she didn't want. We had our whole lives to figure out all the ways we could have fun.

"Easy," she warned.

"Shh, baby. Not today. Today is about fucking you blind, remember?"

I moved up her body and teased her pussy with the head of my dick. She moaned and arched toward me, but I held her hips down with a forearm across them. This was my show now. "You didn't come in my mouth, baby. Until you do, you don't get my dick."

Sam growled at me, and I laughed. I sat

back on my knees, hauled her hips up, and bent my head to lick her slick folds. Using my thumbs, I spread her wide. Licking. Kissing. Biting. Her clit felt like a marble under my tongue. She had trouble breathing, and tears sparkled in the corners of her eyes.

"Come for me, baby." I put three fingers into her and rubbed against the inner wall of her pussy. She screamed, and my fingers were coated with her juice. I sucked her cream off them and she watched every move. Easing her hips down to the bed, I settled back between her thighs.

"Again." I wanted to taste her hot and fresh. Using my tongue inside her, my fingers worked her clit. Her muscles tightened again, and this time, when her hips surged toward me, I let her fuck my face. I was gonna make her scream over and over and over again.

After she came, I licked her dry and then shoved my dick in. She climaxed again as my balls slapped her ass. Oh, fuck, yeah. Her orgasm felt so good I almost shot my load. The hot, crawling stream started at the base of my spine, filling my balls. But not yet. I was going to brand Sam, fucking her so completely, she'd never be satisfied unless I was buried balls deep.

Long and slow. Fast and hard. She came three more times, screaming my name with each climax, and still I fucked her. Until she cheated. She reached between my legs and grabbed my balls. Then the bitch stuck her finger in my asshole. My back bowed, my balls emptied, and my dick was coated with my scalding cum. I pumped into her hard and fast, shoving her finger deeper each time. Gawddamn, but I didn't think I'd ever stop coming. And Sam came with me, her scream a duet with my howl.

Until two guys kicked in the bedroom door.

ELEVEN

SAM

ONE SECOND I'M SCREAMING my lungs out with the best orgasm I've ever had, and the next I'm on the floor, half shoved under the bed, a very naked Easy standing over me with a pistol in one hand and a big ol' honking hunting knife in the other. I could see two pairs of winter boots standing in the doorway to my bedroom. Crud. I was scared to death that my roommates were about to die.

"Easy?" I brushed his bare calf with my fingertips.

"Who the hell are you?" Brad, the guy who owned the house, sounded half scared but a little mad, too.

"I'm the one with the fucking weapons."

"Uhm, Easy?" I tried again and peeked over the top of the mattress. "Uh, hi, Brad. Craig."

"What the hell, Sam?" Tiffany, my third roommate pushed in between the two guys. I recognized the moment she got a good look at Easy, and I got pissed when she licked her lips and purred, "Well, hello to you, too."

I found Easy's tee shirt on the floor and yanked it on before standing up. "Don't you guys knock?"

"The front door's kicked in," Brad groused.

Craig added, "You were freaking screaming."

"And I can see why." Tiff licked her lips again and I clenched my fist, ready to deck the bimbo. Then Easy laughed.

"Jealous much, babe?"

"Shut up, Easy."

Brad, as he typically did, took over. "When did you get back? Where's your sister and her kids?"

Tiffany wore her "fuck me" face. "And who is *this*?"

Craig rolled his eyes. "Dude, put some pants on."

Tossing the knife to the bed, but keeping the pistol in his hand, Easy retrieved his jeans and dressed with all the grace of a dancer. That pissed me off even more. If I tried to pull on my jeans with one hand, I'd be flopping on the floor like a fish.

"Easy, these are my roommates, Brad, Craig, and Tiffany."

Tiff inhaled and let out a breathy sigh, ensuring her well-endowed chest got noticed. And she fluttered her freaking lashes at him. Easy just watched with this stupid little grin on his face.

"What are you, some sort of bodyguard or something?" Tiff pursed her lips, and I wanted to slap her. "Because you can guard me anytime, gorgeous."

"Sarah was murdered by Noni's father." I dropped that little factoid into the room, and all the flirting stopped while the testosterone ramped up. "Easy and his friends are protecting Jonah and Noni. I just came back to get my stuff and turn in my notice."

Brad and Craig, being typical guys, wanted to fix things. Tiff, being a total tramp, just wanted to get closer to Easy. He might have just fucked me until I was hoarse, but he was a freaking MC biker. He'd probably bend Tiff over the dresser and fuck her standing while we all watched. When she strolled over and touched his bare chest, I was ready to lay into Easy. Until I saw his face. He stared at Tiff's hand then at her. Holy crap! He did scarier-than-shit almost as good as the Nightrider president.

Tiff jerked her hand back like she'd been burned and lowered her eyes, all but whimpering. I flashed on a picture of her with her tail tucked between her legs and going belly up in submission. Huh. It was a nice visual. Then I caught Brad and Craig out of the corner of my eye. Damn if they didn't look like they'd be on the floor with Tiff. The hair on the nape of my neck bristled and goosebumps popped up on my arms.

"We don't need your help." Easy's voice was as cold as the outside temperature. "Get out."

The boys fell all over themselves getting through the door, and Tiff all but peed in her pants as she scrambled after them. My heart did a hard thump-thump and my stomach went all butterflies. Who knew Easy going all macho would make me sit up and take notice? This could be why perfectly intelligent women—like me—went all gaga over bikers. Dark. Dangerous. The ultimate alpha male. And this one turned down the blatant invitation of the most popular girl in Brighton. Dang. I really had to watch my step with Easy because I could trip and fall all over him way too...well...easy.

EASY

DAMN GOOD THING I was a Wolf, with a Wolf's reflexes, otherwise those motherfuckers would be dead. Hell, I shoulda killed 'em on general principles just for interrupting Sam and me. Swear to God I thought *both* of my heads were gonna explode. Sam discovered a couple of my buttons that last go round and pushed them at the same time. Fuck. I couldn't stop the grin. Fuck is right. We were going to. Often.

I also got off on the waves of energy coming

off Sam, all of them stinking of vinegar. She was jealous of the bitch who'd come in with the boys. My wolf was strutting around like he was the top dog. Tiff was a teen-aged boy's wet dream. Long platinum hair, big brown eyes, and tits big enough to fill a bucket. Once upon a time, my dick would have been right happy rubbing between those boobs, but now? She didn't do a damn thing for me. I only wanted Sam, with her long, athletic build, her subtle curves, those firm tits that filled the palms of my hands. She had hair that looked liked I'd combed my fingers through it and blue eyes that told me everything I needed to know about turning her on.

My life was fucking fantastic at the moment. After Dumb, Dumber, and Dimwit left, I watched Sam pull on her clothes. Except she was still wearing my tee shirt. Yeah, my chest was all puffed out about that. She didn't even realize she'd left it on. I had an extra in the Hummer. In the meantime, I just wore my cut. Wolves run hot so the winter air didn't faze me. I offered to help Sam pack up, but after she glared at me, I backed off. She had a system, and I'd mess it up. Flopping on the bed, I watched her, and damn if I wasn't hard as steel after she bent over the second time.

I made a list of all the ways I was gonna fuck her. On her hands and knees. Bent over a desk, table, counter, couch—hell, it didn't matter. And on her knees, sucking me off. I wanted her lips around my dick. I was gonna fuck her on my bike too, her sweet thighs griping me as I pounded into her. Ah, hell. What a picture. Sam, wearing my property patch and leather chaps with nothing underneath either piece. Driving down the highway with her in front of me, my dick in her pussy, throbbing with the power of my shovelhead Harley. Swear to God I almost blew my wad right then. That was a fantasy I planned to whack off to any time I couldn't fuck Sam.

She took about an hour, but she'd packed up all her stuff. She wanted to take her skis, but I reminded her she wouldn't need them in Missouri.

"These cost me a month's pay. I am *not* leaving them here."

"Babe, if you head to the ski slopes again, I'll buy you a new pair."

She snapped her mouth shut and glared. "These cost fifteen hundred dollars."

"So." I dug in my pocket and pulled out some cash. I counted off fifteen hundred dollar bills and held them out to her. Her eyes got huge, and she gulped a couple of times. I pictured my dick in her mouth while she did that, and it throbbed and jerked. Oh, yeah. This woman needed to give me a BJ like *now*.

"Where did you get...? No. Never mind. I stand less chance of being arrested if I don't know."

"Naw. This is clean money. I'm a bounty hunter when I'm not dealing with club business. I make some heavy bucks."

"Oh."

I finally got her junk loaded in the Hummer. She took her time saying goodbyes until I got pissed.

"Time to go, babe." I threw her over my shoulder and carried her to the Hummer, stuffed her in the passenger seat, all while listening to her blister my ears with her outrage. She was cute. Like an angry kitten.

Taking the time to pull on another tee shirt from my kit in the backseat, I settled behind the steering wheel, and we headed out of town. Sam was still pouting. I turned on the radio to hide the silence. She'd get over it. She was my mate, whether she knew it or not. And that meant I'd have to explain what I was sooner than later. Yeah, silence was a good thing.

🐾🐾🐾🐾

AFTER STOPPING FOR FOOD, I headed east on I-80 from Cheyenne. Denver was under a blizzard warning, and if we humped it, we could clear the storm somewhere in Nebraska. We'd been driving a couple of hours when she finally looked at me.

"I need a rest stop."

"'Kay. I'll pull off the road."

"Are you kidding me? I want a bathroom not a bush."

I kept driving. Official rest stops were few and far between on this stretch of interstate. We finally hit the outskirts of a town. There was a bar right off the exit.

"There! Stop. Right now."

I looked over. Her hands were fisted on her crossed legs. Huh. She must really need to piss so I did as she asked. She was out of the Hummer before I got it in Park. Shit. She had a really bad habit of doing that. I followed at a jog, but she was just disappearing into a back hallway as I pushed through the crowded room behind her. I caught up as she hit the ladies' room door. I leaned up against the wall, waiting. And watching. Our entrance had attracted a lot of attention.

"Oh hell no. She couldn't piss in the woods beside the road. No, had to come into this shitty excuse for a bar." A bush was cleaner, which Sam figured out as soon as she ducked into the john, trying to hold her breath. By the time she finished, five guys blocked the door to the main room. She pressed against my back and peeked under my arm.

"I'd like to get out of here. Preferably in one piece."

"You and me both, babe." No one ever

accused her of being the queen of understatement. "Stick close. Unless I say run." I'd go fuckin' furry on their asses if I had to.

"Easy?"

"Just do as I say, baby."

I walked forward, Sam dogging my steps. When the assholes didn't move, I let my wolf out to play a little—a shift in the eyes, a hint of tooth in my snarl. Just enough to back them up and open a path to the exit. The bouncer appeared, a lead pipe tucked against one massive shoulder. Shit. Friend or foe?

He looked me up and down then flicked his gaze at Sam before sliding it away to glance at the five guys standing between us. The music stopped and seconds later, so did the buzz of conversation. He didn't raise his voice, but everyone heard him. "Boss wants no trouble with the Nightriders."

"Smart man." Not an enemy then.

"Woman. And yeah, she is." He stepped closer to the five assholes. "Make a hole." They did. He turned sideways to let us pass. "There's the door."

He covered our backs until we were in the Hummer and headed out of the parking lot. I looked over at Sam and said, "Next time—"

"Won't be one. I'm not peeing until we get home."

I didn't remind her it was still a six-hour

drive.

"Easy?"

"What?"

"I had your back."

"Sure you did."

She placed a wicked hunting knife—one that wasn't mine—on the console. Okay, she did have my back. Color me impressed, though I should have figured she was tough given her initial appearance at the clubhouse. Gravedigger made sure her pistol remained there, and I damn sure wanted to know where the fuck she'd gotten the damn knife.

TWELVE

SAM

SINCE COMING BACK from Utah, life settled into some semblance of normal, if living in the clubhouse of a motorcycle gang—er, club, as Easy reminded me constantly—could be defined as *normal* in anyone's dictionary. The kids were off limits to the majority of Nightrider members and the club whores. The Russian laid down a decree—one enforced by the men who I'd finally identified as the inner cadre.

The guy called Hardass, or Hardy, was the vice president. Gravedigger, tall and almost as scary as the Russian, was the sergeant at arms. The Russian snapped his fingers and Digger got it done. Technically, I guess he was the enforcer. I instigated a don't ask, don't tell policy the moment I laid eyes on him, realized he had a gun in his hand, and would shoot me without batting an eye.

Repo and Radar were the secretary and treasurer, which was weird. Why would a criminal outfit like the Nightriders need minutes and financial statements? That left Easy. He said he was road captain, whatever the heck that meant. He mostly backed up Gravedigger and that gave me pause. I knew Easy had blood on his hands, but since I wanted to kill the man who had murdered my sister, I didn't have room to talk. Still, I didn't know what to think about a man who killed easily.

Sunny had taken the kids to the movies, and I was at a loss for something to do, especially after I'd overheard Gravedigger laying down the law to Easy.

"You need to put your patch on her, Easy."

"I know."

"But she doesn't."

"I haven't had the chance to tell her yet."

"Fuck, man. She's in your bed every night."

As I was the one mostly sharing Easy's bed, they had to be talking about me. I knew what wearing his patch meant. I'd be his property. Sunny and Ginger both wore either vests or jackets—depending on the weather—with the property patch. A few other women had them, too. They didn't hang around much, though. The inner cadre treated me differently than the other guys did. It's like they figured I already belonged to Easy so it was hands off. The general membership and prospects weren't so nice about it. They leered and made lewd comments unless Easy was standing there. Those asshats didn't worry me. I could take care of myself.

Easy was out in the garage working on his motorcycle. I finally got the story of how he'd been hurt and ended up on Sarah's doorstep. I'd almost quit blaming him for the Bastard having found and murdered her because of him. It's hard to stay pissed when the man gives you screaming orgasms every night. I wandered into the kitchen and grabbed a couple of beers from the fridge, figuring I'd take one out to him. Maybe he'd take a little break and spend some time with me. I was bored. I worked for a living and being on ski patrol meant I worked hard. Here, I just hung around, and it sucked.

A north wind swirled through the empty yard between the main clubhouse and the two buildings behind it—the garage and the Barracks. I should have made loco coco—hot chocolate and peppermint schnapps—instead of bringing cold beers, but Easy probably wouldn't care. It was the thought, anyway. I ducked through the entrance and stopped dead in my tracks. Then I locked the door.

Easy, hands jammed into his pockets, the action pulling the waistband of his jeans lower on his hips, stood across the room. His bare chest gleamed with sweat, and his tats looked like they'd been oiled. I refrained from licking my lips and swallowed the little moan wedged in my throat. Damn but this man did it for me. And then some. I had to be certifiably insane. Bad enough the Nightriders had taken over my life and those of my sister's kids out of some sense of...what? Gratitude? Honor? Sarah *had* saved Easy's life, and it was a rival gang that murdered her. Now my life was upside down. And my hormones cheered like boy band fangirls.

He kicked the steel drum next to him, all the while staring at the parts strewn on the concrete floor. The motor of his Harley was in pieces. I set the bottles down on the work bench before I squatted and touched several. "Fixing one of these is like making love."

He choked, and I felt his gaze like a physical touch. Looking up, I recognized the hunger in his eyes. It matched my own. Every time I got within ten feet of this man, I wanted to lie down, spread my legs, and fuck him.

After several deep breaths, one dimple came out as he asked, "Yeah?"

"Oh, yeah. Here. I'll show you." I picked up the piston and pushed it into the cylinder head, hiding my grin at his sharp intake of breath.

"Fuck, baby."

And wasn't that the idea? "It goes in like this. You know what I mean?"

He growled at me. "Dammit, Sam. You're killin' me, woman."

"Not yet I'm not." I licked my lips and smiled.

Before I could react, he reached for me, intending to sling me over his shoulder. "Bed. Now."

I loved when he got all growly, but I had a different scenario in mind.

EASY

SAM STOOD THERE just out of my reach, all big-eyed and innocent before she sank to her knees. What the fuck was she—oh holy hell. Her fingers fumbled with the buttons on my jeans. I'd been freakin' hard since the moment she walked through the door and yeah, call me a sumbitch, but my dick in her mouth occupied my thoughts all the damn time. I knocked her hands out of the way and all but ripped my jeans open. Thank fuck I'd gone commando. She cupped my balls, face lowered as she studied my dick.

"Damn, baby, you are fuckin' killin' me here."

She tilted her head back, stared up at me, and licked her lips. "Good."

I groaned. Or growled. Or something. My dick jerked in her hand, its head already coated in pre-cum. She licked it off, and I had to lock my knees. Fuckin' A.

"Suck me, Sam. Do it fucking now." I grabbed her head as she opened her mouth, and I rammed my dick between her lips. She gagged and I backed off. Barely. She wasn't a club whore. She was Sam. She was mine. My mate. Even if she didn't know it yet. She caught her breath then sucked me in again. Her tongue wrapped around the shaft. I had to hold my breath, but I steadied and mumbled a "sorry" when my hips pushed toward her.

I managed to loosen my grip on her hair. For a minute at least. Hot damn fuck a duck, the woman could give head. She sucked me deep, squeezed my balls, and worked the hell out my dick. When she circled the base with her other hand like a cock ring, I thought the top of my head was gonna blow off. Both heads. "Gawddamn, baby."

She laughed. She fuckin' laughed at me. Enough of that shit. I was through playin' around. I held her head still again and pumped into her pretty mouth. I was gonna kiss that mouth after I came in it, was gonna taste my cum on her lips. She didn't fight me. She took everything I had. Fuckin' hell, I could stand here all day rocking into her like this. I loved eating her pussy, and I'd be double-damn sure to repay the favor, but for now, I just let the sensations of her wet lips and her hot mouth rule me.

She gripped the root of my dick in one fist, squeezing in time with her mouth sucking me deep. Her other hand still played with my balls, alternately rolling them and cupping them. My sac stretched tight, and heat stabbed at the base of my spine. The hand on my balls dropped away, and I growled until I saw what she was doing. She dipped that hand into the front of her jeans, pushed it between her legs.

Holy shit but I wanted to strip her naked and watch her touching her pussy while she sucked my dick. Then her hand reappeared. Her middle finger all but dripped with her juices. My balls drew up, and I was fucking close to shooting my load. My fingers tangled in her hair, and I sped up the rhythm. I thought she was going to cup my balls again, but she didn't. She pushed that finger, hot and slick from being inside her, into my ass. Deep. I saw fucking stars as I spewed.

She gulped me down, even when I kept coming and coming. I wasn't gentle when I jerked Sam to her feet. I took her mouth like she'd taken my dick. Hot and hard. Tasting myself on her lips was better than rare steak, was almost as good as tasting her on my lips.

Sam pushed against my chest, squirmed away, and backed up putting space between us. She smirked at me. She fuckin' smirked at me. I didn't know what that word meant until I looked at her in this moment.

"Bitch."

"Yeah, I am."

THIRTEEN

EASY

WHAT'S THAT BULLSHIT about making plans and life? I stood at the edge of the clearing and watched Sam. She wanted to run. The urge was obvious in the way she stood and the whiffs of scorched hair I picked up just confirmed it. Panic. Given the situation, if I were her, I'd run too.

Thing is, Sam wouldn't get far. I'd hunt her down. My wolf was furious and stalking just beneath the surface of my skin. Ducking her head, she hunched her shoulders and turned partly away, watching me from the corners of her eyes. Her chest rose and fell and the stench of her fear and panic turned my wolf frantic.

When I set up this deal, I'd wanted her to see the stars fall out of the atmosphere. The Leoneid meteor shower out here away from the lights of Kansas City was an amazing sight. I wanted to make love to her, beneath the shooting stars. I wanted to take her to my idea of heaven, leaving everyone behind but us. Just us. Sam and me. I would have explained what I am, and what she means to me, what she is to me. And then I would claim her. My mate. And she'd wear my patch so every gawddamned Nightrider knew she was my property.

Like a moonstruck idiot, I'd agreed to let her drive out here to meet me. She had something to take care of down in town with Sunny, and I was thinking I'd be all romantic and shit. I came early to set up things—a blanket, food. I built a fire pit to help chase the cold and even had a bottle of wine for her, one that was expensive as fuck, but she was worth it. Hell, I'd even bought her fucking flowers. I was going to give them to her when I asked her to wear my patch. I had a leather jacket made with the Nightrider patch and PROPERTY OF EASY on the back.

Then that gawddamned Hell Dog showed up. He'd followed me, thought he could take me out.

Nothing hunts in the wild better than a Wolf. The Dog parked down the road, tried to sneak up on me by coming through the woods. Yeah, like I'd let that fucking happen. I faded back, stripped, and shifted. I took him out in wolf form. Wasn't much of a fight. I chewed his hand off before he could pull the trigger on his gun. Then I ripped out his throat. His blood tasted copper-penny sharp and the rusty scent of it filled my lungs.

Sam arrived and caught me shifting from wolf to man. I hadn't meant for her to find out what I was this way. That's what all this romantic crap was for. Sunny told me I needed to court her, show her I could be civilized. I'm a fucking Wolf. And a Nightrider. Civilized isn't part of our vocabulary.

I stood there, the Hell Dog's blood smeared on my chest and face. Bad enough she'd seen me in wolf form, but now there was the fucking body too. I needed to distract her, draw her away, leave the damn evidence far behind so she'd forget. Yeah, right. I wiped my face with my arm and hoped I got most of the blood off. She just stood there staring at me, eyes wide, mouth hanging open. I walked toward her.

"Sam..." I reached for her, but she backed away a step. Her eyes flicked from me to the dead guy.

"Could you at least put clothes on?" Her voice sounded tinny.

"You've seen me naked before."

"Dammit, Easy. Don't make this so hard."

The look on her face hurt. "I didn't want you to find out like this."

"Find out like *this*? Oh my god, Easy. You killed him. And...the w-wolf. I stood here and watched that wolf turn into y-you. A very naked you."

"Yeah, well, fur doesn't just turn into clothes. It doesn't work like that. This isn't magic."

"What are you?" Disgust—and fear—coated her voice. I quit breathing through my nose, my wolf overwhelmed by so many contradictory smells.

"There's a technical term for it. *Lupi versi pellis.* It's...aw hell, baby." I scrubbed my thighs with fisted hands to keep from grabbing her. "It's in my DNA."

"That's..." She inhaled a ragged breath. "This is just crazy, Easy."

"Yeah, guess it would be to some people."

"Some people?" Her voice rose as she edged toward hysteria. "Try everyone, Easy. This is just fucking crazy! I'm crazy. Or drugs. A hallucination. That's it. I—"

I couldn't blame her. I scrubbed a hand through my hair before I realized I'd probably smeared more blood. I bent over, snatched the blanket and used it to clean off before hitching it around my hips. I had a raging hard-on from the adrenaline rush and my mate standing here smelling like prey.

"You aren't crazy, baby. And you didn't imagine it."

Her gaze skittered around, looking everywhere but at me. "So do you like...turn into a wolf and howl at the full moon? Or eat people?"

"I only eat you, baby." And that was the dumbest thing to ever come out of my mouth. I was making jokes because I didn't know what else to do.

"Get dressed, Easy." Her voice held no inflection this time.

Without letting her out of my sight, I rooted around in the woods. I found my clothes, and pulled on my jeans and boots. Walking to the Hummer, I replaced my cut with a leather jacket and grabbed another blanket—a clean one without blood. When I stopped in front of Sam to wrap her in it, she snatched it from my hands and backed away.

I gestured toward the big log I'd pulled up near the fire pit. "Sit down, Sam. I'll answer any questions you have."

"Can I leave?"

No! My wolf growled, and I fought for control. "Yeah. But I wish you'd stay." I hunkered down to light the fire. I could see the small shivers trembling across her hands from the cold. "We need to talk this through. There are things you need to understand. About me. You. What I am. What you are."

"What I am? What the hell are you talking about, Easy? I'm me. I'm human. You...aren't. You're some kind of...crazy...something. I don't even know what to call you." She glanced toward the body lying at the edge of the woods. "Except cold-blooded killer."

"Yeah, I killed the motherfucker, Sam. He's wearing Hell Dog colors. He followed me out here. When my wolf took him down, he had a fucking gun in his hand ready to shoot me. That's self-defense under the rule of law. What if he'd killed me instead? And took you." Oxygen turned to concrete in my chest as I said the words. My biggest fear danced in the flames of the fire—that something would happen to Sam. "I'd kill the asshole again— fuck, I'd kill any man who hurt you. Do you understand that? I would ride through the fires of hell to keep you safe. You are everything to me, Sam. Every fucking thing."

"No. Don't go there, Easy."

"Too late, baby. You want to know what I am? I'm a Wolf, and Wolves mate for life."

She settled, finally. Asked more questions. I answered as honestly as I could. Information about Wolves and the Nightriders was on a need-to-know basis. She needed to know, but until she wore my patch, until she agreed to be my mate, I couldn't answer everything.

We talked until the stars no longer fell, until night turned to day, the gray fingers of dawn peeking over the horizon to chase shadows across the landscape. The fire burned down to embers, the snap and pop of the cooling coals breaking the silence stretching between us. She left without saying goodbye. I couldn't leave what I was behind to go after her. Alone, I shifted, raised my muzzle and howled. I'd lost her, and no matter how many stars I wished on, she was gone.

FOURTEEN

SAM

I drove like a crazypants race-car driver on meth, and I was freaking lucky there wasn't a cop between me and Mission Springs. I'm not sure why I automatically headed back to the Nightriders' clubhouse. It wasn't home. Except...it was. That's where Jonah and Noni were, where Easy was. My chest hurt, and it was still difficult to draw a deep breath. What was wrong with me? The guy was a freaking *monster*! A werewolf. Or something. Holy crap.

Waiting at a traffic light, I started shaking and couldn't stop. I managed to pull around the corner and into an empty parking lot. It was still early morning though traffic picked up while I sat there reviewing everything Easy had said.

I couldn't become a werewolf. Wolf shifter. Whatever! Bodily fluids, bites, nothing would infect me. Only what he had wasn't an infection. It was inherent in his damn DNA. He was born that way. Hyperventilating, I rested my forehead on the steering wheel of my Jeep until I could breathe normally again. Whatever alien *thing* he carried inside him, it was passed on with the Y chromosome. But not every little boy born to someone like him had the ability to shift.

Easy and babies? Why would my mind even go there? I already have two to take care of, I wasn't married, and I damn sure wasn't having monster babies! A full-body shudder racked me. My cheeks were wet from tears I didn't realize I was crying. When had Easy wormed his way so deeply into my heart?

He was a bastard. And a major asshat. But Jonah and Noni loved him, and he was so gentle with them. Yeah, he roughhoused with Jojo, but he never let the boy get hurt. In fact, all the Nightrider officers took special care of the kids. The rest of the members? Not so much, but they mostly ignored the kids because they knew the wrath of the Russian, Hardy, Gravedigger, Repo, and Radar would fall on their heads. Heck, Easy was even quicker to jump on people, especially the club whores when the kids were around. He took special care to keep the kids away from the darker stuff that went on.

Being honest with myself, I admitted Easy took special care of the kids, period. He built the door between their room and his, where I spent every night. If one of the kids didn't feel good or had a nightmare, Easy got up and went to them. Most times, I didn't even know until I woke up and realized he was gone. I scrubbed at my face with the heels of my hands. I didn't know what to do. Self-preservation dictated I grab the kids and run like hell. Except the Hell Dogs were still out there. 'Cause d'uh. Dead one on top of Sweetheart Hill.

I had nowhere to go. No job. Not much money in the bank. And no way to take care of the kids—or keep them safe. Jonah's father had been found in his police car, apparently dead of natural causes though the last news report said his autopsy was pending. Not that I'd have gone to him anyway.

There was relief in the fact I wouldn't have to fight him for Jonah's custody. Which left the Bastard, who was still out there. Sarah had been stupid to put his name on Noni's birth certificate, and if he had a copy, he could cause serious problems. If I couldn't afford groceries, I sure couldn't afford an attorney to fight a custody battle.

With no choice but to suck it up, I wiped my face, started the Jeep, and headed for the clubhouse. I'd just stay out of everyone's way, and away from Easy. If he got pushy, maybe I could talk Repo and Sunny into making him stay away from me and the kids. If not, we'd just stay behind locked doors whenever Easy was around. He wasn't always at the clubhouse. He worked as a bounty hunter, or sometimes as a bouncer at some bar the Nightriders owned. And he'd been assigned to what was mysteriously referred to as "the night shift." When I complained about his long absences, he explained he was taking extra jobs for the money. So he could buy us a house.

And remembering that is all it took. I was boo-hooing again and had to find another parking lot. Ten minutes later, I got myself under control enough I could drive. Rush hour traffic hit, and it took me almost an hour to get back to the clubhouse. The guys on the gate let me in, grinning hugely until they got a look at me. Then both of them sobered up, their expressions morphing into narrowed glares. I drove around back to the parking area wondering what I'd done now, and found Jonah and Noni watching Repo put something together.

I used a wet wipe to wash my face, but my eyes were still red-rimmed. I climbed out of the Jeep and headed over to find out what was going on. Noni was ear-to-ear grins, and Jonah looked pretty pleased too.

"Aunt Sam! Look! A fort." Jonah bounced on his toes.

There was a big pile of wood, a couple of swings, and other paraphernalia for a kid-friendly play set. Repo glanced over his shoulder, a big smile on his face for about two seconds. His expression turned carefully blank. What was going on?

"Where'd all this stuff come from?"

"Easy got it for us, Aunt Sam."

Easy. Again. Looking after my kids.

"You okay, hon?"

Noni had wrapped around my leg, and I pried her loose to pick her up. I glanced at Repo over her head. "Yeah. I'm fine."

He studied me for a minute before shrugging and returning to work. Something was definitely going on, but I was too stressed out to figure out what it was.

Jonah finally picked up on my mood, and he stared at me, even going behind me to stare at my jacket. "Aunt Sam? Where's Easy?"

"He's not back yet?"

He shook his head. "Nope. Miss Sunny said you guys would be gone awhile because Easy was doing something special for you, and you guys would be doin'...stuff."

"Jonah!" How would he know about...*stuff*?

Speaking of Sunny... The woman barreled across the grass, all smiles and excitement until she skidded to a stop in front of me. A small vee creased the skin between her eyebrows as she spun me around.

"Where is it?"

"Where's what?" I had no clue what she

was talking about.

"The jacket."

"What jacket?"

Her eyes went wide. "Didn't Easy ask you?" Sunny leaned closer and got a good look at my face. "Sam? Have you been crying? What's wrong?" She glanced around, her expression morphing from happy anticipation to concerned. "Where's Easy?"

"I don't know where he is. Why is everyone giving me the fish eye this morning?"

"Last night. Didn't Easy ask you?"

"Dammit, Sunny. Ask me what?"

Her face fell. "Oh no."

Something was obviously wrong. "You'd better tell me right now what's going on, Sunny."

Repo glared at her, but she shrugged as if to say, "What am I supposed to do?" She inhaled a couple of times then reached for Noni. Putting her on the grass next to Jonah, she told the kids to help Repo and gestured for me to step away.

"Honey, what went wrong? Easy had plans for last night."

How could I tell her that Easy was a freak of nature, that he could change into a wolf and chew the hand off a man, could rip out a human's throat. Instead of answering, I just stared at her.

"Easy had it all planned. He had your

jacket custom made. He even bought flowers because Ginger said you'd think they were romantic. He was going to ask you to wear his patch. To be...his."

Everything caved in on me at once, and I sank to my knees. I wasn't all that familiar with MC life, but even I knew it was a huge deal when a member offered his patch to a woman. I didn't like the idea of being "property," but after talking it over with Sunny and Ginger, and a couple of the other old ladies, I realized it was tantamount to a proposal and marriage.

If I hadn't seen him change, with all that blood on him, I would have said yes. I would have been tied to a monster. Thank goodness I'd escaped that fate. Even if my heart felt like a dead lump in my chest.

Sunny squatted in front of me and touched my shoulder. "Sam? What happened?" Something in my expression must have leaked my thoughts. "Oh, crap. He showed you his wolf."

I landed on my butt in the grass. "You..." I gulped. "You know what he is?" I had to stay in control so I didn't scare the kids, but my voice wavered between a squeak and a screech.

"Well, d'uh, Sam. We all know." She blinked a couple of times. "Well, not all of us. The human brothers don't know, or the club whores, but those of us mated to Wolves do."

Unable to breathe, sparkles formed before my eyes right before darkness sucked me under.

🐾 🐾 🐾 🐾

I WOKE UP IN BED, completely disoriented. Jonah perched beside me, his expression anxious. Repo sat across the room bouncing Noni on his knee. Sunny walked over and touched Jonah's shoulder.

"See? I told you she was fine. Probably didn't eat breakfast, s'all. Why don't you and Noni go back outside and help Repo put your fort together, 'kay?"

Jonah touched my arm as if to reassure himself that I was there. "Are you okay, Aunt Sam?"

"Yeah, Jojo. I'm fine." I lied—I wasn't fine at all—but what could I tell him that would make sense? I patted his knee and gestured toward Repo with my head. "Go on back outside. I know you're excited to get the fort built. Maybe Repo can draft some help so it goes faster."

"Yeah, I can do that. C'mon, boy." Repo stood up and tucked a giggling Noni under his arm. The ease with which some of these men handled the children just blew me away, especially since they didn't seem to have any of their own.

Repo shut the door behind them, and I

looked around. This wasn't the room I shared with Easy. I'd been carried to the kids' room and put on Jonah's bed. I glanced over at Sunny and sucked in my breath. She looked furious, hands fisted on her hips, chin jutting aggressively beneath a slash of tightly pressed lips and narrowed eyes.

This was Sunny—bright, sweet...sunny. She never got angry.

"What the hell is going on with you, Sam?"

"With me? Holy crap, Sunny. Easy changed from a wolf to a man covered in blood."

"Wait! What? Is Easy hurt?" Her anger melted into concern.

"What? No. Easy ripped the throat out of a guy. He said it was a Hell Dog. I didn't go over to look."

"A Hell Dog? A Hell Dog was up on Sweetheart Hill? Why didn't Easy call? The club needs to know that. And he hasn't come back. He's gonna be in so much trouble."

"Wait. I just said Easy changed from a wolf into a man and you freak because a Hell Dog was there? Why aren't you freaked about the whole wolf to man thing?"

Sunny stared at me like I'd grown a second head. "Why would I freak out? Repo does it all the time. He's a Wolf too."

My heart thudded, and I thought I might pass out again. Repo was one of the monsters, and at that very moment, he had my kids. I must have said something to that effect because all the sudden, Sunny slapped me. Hard. My cheek stung from the blow and when I touched it, I could feel a raised welt in the shape of her hand.

"You bitch!" Her eyes filled with tears, and now she looked like I'd ripped the heart out of a puppy or something. "How could you say that? After everything we've done for you. You don't know shit, Samantha. And you damn sure don't deserve Easy. God. He must be heartbroken. No wonder he hasn't come back. Everyone knew he was giving you his patch. It's a huge deal like getting married. Only with the Wolves, it means even more. Wolves mate for life."

She flicked a tear off her cheek and stomped across the room before turning to face me again. "You know what? To hell with you. Why don't you just pack up all your crap and get the fuck out. We'll take care of the kids. You don't deserve Easy and you don't deserve them."

The door slammed behind her, and I just sat there, stunned. How was Easy the good guy in all this? What did I do wrong? I stared at the door, expecting Sunny to come back in and apologize and tell me we'd go share some mocha ice cream in the kitchen and talk about our men. Only she didn't, and an ominous silence enveloped the whole compound.

FIFTEEN

SAM

EASY DIDN'T COME BACK. Three days,
going on four now. I mostly stayed in the kids'
room, sharing Noni's bed with her. I only
went downstairs or over to the kitchen in the
clubhouse at the butt-crack of dawn when
everyone was either passed out or had gone
home. Most of the guys lived off property and
all the married couples had houses. Easy once
mentioned he had a one-bedroom apartment,
but the inner circle all had quarters in the
Barracks. There were other rooms where the
members could shack up with their whores or
pass out and sleep through their hangovers.

The first time I ran into one of the
Nightriders in the clubhouse, he backed me
up against the wall and tried to feel me up. I
kneed him in the balls and ran back to our
room. I was scared, but mostly pissed. None
of the members had ever disrespected me like
that. Then I remembered. I wasn't Easy's girl
anymore. But the Russian had told them I
wasn't a club whore. Had he rescinded his
order because I'd turned Easy down?

Confronting him to ask did not seem like a bright idea under the circumstances.

After that nightmare encounter, I stayed out of sight. Jonah was a smart kid, and he figured out real quick that I was in some kind of trouble with the MC. He sneaked peanut butter and jelly sandwiches to me and bottles of water. I never heard any noise in Easy's room, and the one time I tried the doors, they were both locked.

Noni's nightmares came back, and she'd cry out for Easy. One hit just as I was sneaking out to dash to the bathroom. Since I couldn't get into Easy's room, I had to use the communal one down the hall. I sure wasn't going to pee, much less shower, with freaking bikers wandering around. I came back to bed, and held her in my arms. Her sobbing plea for Easy shredded my heart. Rocking her in the dark was a light-bulb moment. Easy wouldn't return as long as I was here. If I left, he'd come back, and Noni would feel safe again. She was only three, but she trusted Easy more than she trusted me.

"Shh, Noni. It'll be okay. Aunt Sam is gonna fix it. Easy will be here soon. Go back to sleep, baby girl."

I rocked her until she cried herself to sleep. Tucking her in, I gathered up my stuff, wrote a quick note to Jonah explaining why and how to reach me if he or Noni needed anything. With a heavy heart, I slipped out. It was time for me to leave.

GRAVEDIGGER

I HEARD THE BITCH stumble downstairs. She was doing her best to sneak around, but she sounded like a herd of buffalo. She'd been raiding the kitchen around this time every night so I waited for her, standing back in the shadows. She skulked by and was silhouetted in a window seconds later. I recognized the shape of a backpack slung over one of her shoulders. Where the fuck did she think she was going?

Her scent washed over me, and I almost sneezed. Ammonia. Burnt toast. Pepper sauce. The bitch was definitely conflicted. I expected fear and maybe anger, but determination? I probably should have anticipated that, too, based on the crap Easy said about her.

Fuck. Easy. No one had seen or heard from him since Sam came back alone. I'd gone to the hill, saw the traces of his kill. He'd cleaned up after himself, but then disappeared. The only fresh scents were his, the bitch's, the Hell Dog's. He left under his own steam, but unless he was dead or mortally wounded, he should have returned to the clubhouse. Russki was beyond pissed.

At least I'd make money on this deal.

Hollywood owed me a hundred. I thought it was a sucker bet when I made it because he figured the bitch would run before now. Hardy, in wolf form, prowled out in the yard. We didn't care if she left, but she damn sure wasn't taking the kids out of here. I voted to kill her, but Repo, Hardy, and Radar overruled me. It would upset the kids and truthfully, I didn't want to rip out Easy's heart any more than it already had been.

I knew all about that heart ripping thing. I'd lived without mine for years now. Whoever said time heals all wounds was full of shit. My chest still felt empty. I stuffed my memories away when the lock clicked on the back door. It creaked as Sam pulled it open and headed outside.

Watching through the window, I picked up a shadow of movement near the garage. Hardy. Sam unlocked her Jeep, tossed the backpack in. She turned to stare up at the window of the room where the kids stayed, and the mercury security light caught her in its pale orange glow. Her expression was despondent, as if she'd not only lost her puppy, but also discovered it had been eaten by wolves. I almost laughed. She'd been nothing but trouble, but she was Easy's mate. He was my brother, and I worried for him. Been there. Done that. Burned the fucking tee shirt. The bitch swiped at her cheeks with the back of her hand. Crying. What the fuck did she have to cry about? She mounted up and started the Jeep. Huh. Maybe she'd grown a brain, and was smart enough to leave the kids here where we could keep them safe.

The two-way radio on my belt clicked. Repo. "Kids are still asleep."

"She's headed toward the gate. I'll radio down for them to let her go."

Yeah, the sooner she was gone, the sooner Easy would come back to the club and life could get back to normal. Well, as normal as possible with two little kids living in the Barracks, the Hell Dogs bent on killing every last Nightrider, and a Blood Moon on the horizon.

SAM

I DIDN'T GET FAR. I couldn't. I made it as far as Lawrence, Kansas a little over an hour later in the predawn traffic. I stopped to get coffee, and when I got back on I-70, I was headed eastbound. I couldn't abandon the kids. The Nightriders wouldn't let me back into the compound, but I'd stay close enough I could watch Jojo and Noni through binoculars or something. And what would happen if Easy didn't come back?

Was that even possible? Didn't he owe some sort of allegiance to the Nightriders? Could he just pick up and leave and not look back? I shook so hard at that thought I had to pull over to the side of the highway. I breathed through the panic attack.

God, I missed him. Missed him all the way deep in my bones. Thinking about him hurt. Not thinking about him hurt even worse. But he was a freaking werewolf. Only he said he wasn't. He was something else. Something... other.

Whatever that "other" was didn't bother Sunny. She married Repo. And Repo was the same... *thing* as Easy. Goosebumps popped up on my arms, and I kicked the heater up a couple of notches. Some of the Nightriders gave off an energy that people picked up on, even if they didn't know why. Easy. Repo. Radar. Hardy. I shivered like a whole coven of witches danced on my grave. That meant Digger and the Russian were Wolves too. I flashed on a picture of Noni riding the Russian piggyback, of Jonah in the garage with Easy and Repo as they rebuilt Easy's Harley. Noni patting Easy's cheeks and making kissy faces at him.

And I remembered what the Russian had said to me when he issued his decree concerning the kids.

"The man who would claim Noni is my enemy. She is under my personal protection. I will kill anyone—anyone—who tries to take her. Do you understand, Samantha Prescott?"

He hadn't been talking about just Noni. And it wasn't just because the Bastard was a Hell Dog and, therefore, an enemy of the Nightriders. Most of the members could care less about the kids, a few probably despised them. But the inner circle? The cadre of officers? They all doted on the children and not in a creepy, weird uncle way. They truly cared about Jonah and Noni. Like a wolf pack cared for their young. And their mated females.

They treated the club whores like what they were—women who would do anything to be noticed by club members. Women who thought they could fuck their way to a property patch. But the women who wore those patches? They were treated with respect. Protected. Even the real assholes in the club acted differently toward them.

Easy. He'd lured me up to that place to...well, hell. Basically to propose to me. Marriage wasn't something MCs did as a rule, though both Sunny and Ginger wore rings.

Wolves mate for life.

Easy's words. And Sunny's. They were branded in my memory. I rested my forehead against the steering wheel. Would Easy come after me? I doubted it, considering he'd disappeared after that fiasco on Sweetheart Hill, and despite his declarations. Did I even want him to track me down?

A hard rap on the window made me scream. Heart beating so fast I thought I might pass out, I stared. Uniform. Slate blue. Smokey Bear hat. I swallowed. A state trooper. I managed to roll down the window.

"Are you all right, miss?"

I nodded, not trusting my voice. My fingers closed on my cell phone, and I held it up. "I'm sorry. I...a phone call. I pulled off to take it. Isn't that what I'm supposed to do?"

His expression remained skeptical. "Are you sick?" His gaze narrowed on my eyes. Hell. He thought I was high.

"I'm fine, sir. Do you need my driver's license?"

"Utah plates on the vehicle. You're a long way from home."

Damn, did he think my Jeep was stolen or something? "I live in Brighton, Utah. I'm headed to Mission Springs to see my niece and nephew." How much could I reveal and not have everything fall apart?

"Driver's license, registration, and proof of insurance please, ma'am."

My paperwork was all in order, thankfully. He let me go with the admonition that I had thirty days to get a Missouri ID if I stuck around, but he'd let the Missouri authorities worry about my legality. I thanked him, got control of my emotions, started the Jeep, put it in gear, and got the hell out of there.

First things first. I needed to find a place close to the compound, but far enough away I wouldn't be seen by the Nightriders and wouldn't be caught by the Hell Dogs.

EASY

I WATCHED THE STRIPPER work the pole and didn't give a fuck. I was on my tenth straight whiskey and even without watered-down booze I'd still have been stone-cold sober. Wolf metabolism sucked. So did my life. I hadn't slept in five nights now, but I wasn't so far gone I didn't recognize the Wolf energy crashing through the room.

Gravedigger appeared on one side, Hardass on the other.

"Damn, Easy. That's one ugly bitch."

"Yeah, Digger. She's just your type."

The sonavabitch laughed and tossed the dancer a twenty when she scowled at his comment. Hardy grabbed my glass and sniffed.

"Fuck, man. This shit will burn out your stomach lining."

"How many titty bars did it take you to find me?

"Too many." Hardy winked at Digger when he added, "That last nudie joint offers breakfast. Gives eggs sunny-side up and hash browns a whole new meaning."

"I guess the Russian is pissed."

Digger snorted. "Or something. It's time to come home, Easy."

"I can't."

"Fuck, Easy. It's not like we'd take you back and hog tie you. Hell, your wolf would just have fun chewing through the ropes anyway."

"Not funny, Hardy."

"She's gone, man. Come back with us. There's nothing to keep you away now."

Gone. Sam really left me. How could she take away everything I am? She took my heart. My soul. And left only the beast within me. The one that howled in the dark because she'd walked away from us—left us alone—on Sweetheart Hill. And wasn't that a crock of shit. Sweet-fucking-heart Hill. I bared all my secrets to her up there under the stars. All the bitch did was squeeze me into dust, wipe any traces of me off her hands, and walk away like I was dog shit on the bottom of her boot.

One of the floor dancers waltzed up to offer us lap dances. She was a redhead with big boobs, just Hardy's type. He ignored her. That meant he was serious about dragging my ass out of here. I didn't want to go. I couldn't deal with Sam's scent lingering everywhere.

Hardy slugged me in the arm. "Dammit, Easy. You need to come back to the compound. Noni's having nightmares again. She cries out, calling for you."

"Sam can deal with it. As she fucking reminded me in no uncertain terms, Jojo and Noni are her kids now." Wait. Maybe I was drunker than I thought. Something didn't add up. Hardy said Sam left. How did he know Noni wanted me? Click. Pieces fell into place. "Fuckin' hell. Are you telling me Sam ran off and left the kids behind?"

I squeezed the glass so hard it shattered in my hand. I was so fucking pissed off that if I ever saw that gawddamned bitch again I would slit her throat. Bad enough she cut me off at the balls, but to leave the kids? They loved her. So did I. And yeah, she'd fucking left me, hadn't she? Why would she stick around for Jonah and Noni?

The bouncer was a little slow on the uptake, but he finally figured out things were tense in our little party and there was blood involved. I was ready to fight the fucker and every other sumbitch in the place. I'd been itching for a bar fight since the day Sam walked away. The one I managed to start didn't count for shit, seeing as it took place half-past dawn and most of the drunks left in the joint could barely stand.

Digger and Hardy marched me outside before I killed somebody. We mounted our Harleys, but just sat there a minute. I was staring at the rest of my life, and it was a fucking black hole without Sam in it.

Hardy stared at me until I focused on him. "Time to start over, Easy."

Oh yeah. Let me get right on that. The only woman who'd ever meant jack shit to me—my fucking mate—thought I was a monster. Starting over would be a piece of cake. I just wanted to drink so damn much whiskey, I could finally pass out. Only problem with that solution was a little blonde girl with haunted blue eyes who needed a Wolf to keep the real monsters away.

SIXTEEN

EASY

CHURCH WAS RUTHLESS, but I took the heat. I'd abandoned my brothers when I disappeared. Russki let me and everyone else know the brutal consequences of my actions. I took the beating from Digger and Hardy and then did a turn under the not-so-tender mercies of the Russian's flogger as the main attraction at Nightshades. I'd heal faster than a human, but getting skin flayed off hurts like hell. Plus, I was on garbage detail for the foreseeable future. I got all the shit assignments, including gate duty just like a fucking prospect.

Thing is, Russki wasn't that pissed about me going MIA. Moonstruck Wolves are pretty much brain dead and he would've cut me some slack. Yeah, I'd still get the beating, but that would have ended the punishment. It was the situation with the Hell Dog that sent him over the edge. With good reason. I didn't report in about being followed, or about killing the motherfucker. I'd screwed up big time by putting my brothers in danger, and I was damn fucking lucky I was still breathing.

I sucked it up. Did my penance. When I wasn't working for the MC, I did my best to get drunk. We hadn't seen Hell Dogs around for more than a week so Sunny and Repo took the kids to their house to stay. The clubhouse and all the shit that went down there was not a place for kids to be living. Besides, Repo and Sunny had a real yard, and there was discussion about Jonah going to school.

Radar was a master forger. He could make documents showing Jonah and Noni belonged to Repo and Sunny. Only problem with that plan was Noni. She called me daddy. In front of everyone. And my fucking heart broke every time I heard the word on her lips.

That'd been my plan. I'd patch Sam. Claim her as my mate. And we'd adopt the kids. All legal and shit. No forgery. Nothing fake. Do it for real. Gawddamn but I loved those kids. I really did. But Sam? Sam fucked up my head. Both of them.

I spent most of my free time in wolf form patrolling Repo's neighborhood. Nobody would get close to my kids. The rest of the time I worked hauling in penny-ante crooks for the bond company or bouncing at Chasin' Tail, the Nightrider-owned strip club. When I wasn't working or sleeping for a couple of hours, I drank to get stupid, not that it helped.

Days and nights rolled together until the ache in my gut that was the memory of Sam turned to ice. I couldn't keep the anger burning any longer. She was gone.

I hated working the fucking door at Tail's. I had nothing to do but look intimidating and think. I damn sure didn't need to do that shit because my thoughts always circled around to Sam, to how wrong I'd been about her.

Digger leaned up against the wall beside me. A bass beat throbbed, and my nose was stuffed with the stench of raw sex.

"How long are you gonna keep playing the waiting game, man?"

"I'm done playin', Digger."

"Yeah? You still look like a pussy-whipped dickwad to me. Ya gotta get out, Easy. Find a willing bitch to spread her legs. If that doesn't appeal, at least find one who'll go on her knees and suck you off. Ain't healthy for a Wolf to go without."

"How long did it take you?"

His eyes narrowed, and I caught a hint of fang in his smile. "To do what? Fuck every whore in the clubhouse?"

Digger didn't talk much, but we all knew there was something in his past haunting him. He was merciless to the club whores, taking sex from them and tossing them away when he was done. He never fucked the same girl twice.

"I got the door. Go get fucked."

He shoved at my shoulder, pushing me off the barstool I'd hitched my hip on. If he was going to take my shift, I had a better idea. There was a bottle behind the bar with my name on it. I snagged it and headed to an empty party room in the back. One of the dancers slinked in a few minutes later.

"Digger sent me." She pouted her lips like that made her look sexy or something. "I'm Lola. And you know what the song says, right?"

What the fuck was she talking about? I caught a whiff of her—cheap perfume and cheaper sex.

She dropped down on the couch beside me and rubbed my zipper. My dick didn't respond. Instead of getting the message, she licked her lips. "Whatever Lola wants, Lola gets, and right now I want you. In my mouth."

I didn't fight her. She got my jeans open and palmed my limp dick. There was only one bitch it wanted to play with and this bimbo wasn't her. Undeterred, she stretched out on the couch, her head in my lap.

Licks. Sucks. Strokes. Playing with my balls. She tried everything. Turned out my dick did have a mind of its own, getting half-way hard, which in a human would be a major woody. She flashed me a look of triumph and really went to work. Maybe Digger was right. What was that saying about getting back on the horse? Only in this case, it was getting back on the whores.

SAM

I'D LEARNED ENOUGH living in the mountains to stay downwind of anything resembling a wild animal. The logical part of my brain still had trouble assimilating the idea that Easy and the rest of them turned into wolves. I kept watch from the safety of an abandoned apartment house. Once I figured out they'd moved the kids to Sunny and Repo's, I discovered the boarded up slum. A pile of junk in the back provided a hiding spot for my Jeep, especially after I threw some tarps over it. I found a second floor apartment where I could see Sunny and Repo's house and had a good view of the whole street. Using a crowbar from the Jeep, I pried just enough boards off the door so I could get in, but the place would still look abandoned. A couple of trips and I had my sleeping bag, camp stove, and ice chest installed. As long as it didn't get too cold, I could camp out here until I got the kids back.

Only I didn't know when that would be. They were happy. And safe. There was always at least one Nightrider around when they were at the house. Sunny acted like their mom. She baked cookies and took them to the nearby park. And when they played there, a silver-black and white wolf with blue eyes always watched them. Just like I did.

The first time I'd seen what I thought was an extraordinarily large Siberian husky, I panicked when Noni ran to the animal and threw her arms around its neck. The wind blew into my face that day, and I clearly heard the little girl.

"Dada. Da! Pay wif me."

Noni patted the dog's cheeks and kissed its nose before darting off in a crazy game of tag. Just like she did with Easy. And this game was a thing every time I followed them to the park. Today was the same.

That time I saw Easy shift from wolf to man, it was after sunset and he'd been in shadows. I didn't get a close look at the wolf, only that there was an animal one minute and the next, a naked Easy stood there with something dark smeared across his chest and face. This is what he looked like in his wolf form. He was beautiful. I could see his blue eyes even from this distance, appreciated how gentle he was, how he tugged the back of Noni's jacket when she got too close to the street and herded her back to Jonah and Sunny. Jojo threw a ball for him to chase and Easy did, over and over, patiently returning to my nephew.

When it came time to say goodbye, he let the kids hug him, and he licked their faces making both of them giggle. Then he trotted off, wild and so beautiful I had to breathe around the constriction in my chest. Breathing at that moment felt like when I'd been skiing hard and furious at high altitudes, sucking in air that stabbed my lungs with cold knives.

I hid behind a dumpster, watching until Sunny and the kids loaded up and drove away. The roar of two motorcycles echoed, following Sunny's Charger. Prospects assigned to guard duty—which they took very seriously. The two men had stood close enough to me I overheard their conversation. Something happened to Easy after I left. Something horrible enough to make an indelible impression on them. I'd just seen Easy's wolf so whatever it was, he'd survived, but at what cost? And was I the cause of his punishment?

Not sure if Easy would hang around in his wolf form, I delayed sneaking back to my temporary place. I trudged to the nearby McDonald's and ordered from the dollar menu, got a giant drink, and settled in to eat and wait. After an hour, I headed out.

Three blocks from the apartment building, the hair on my neck prickled. I tried to check my back trail as surreptitiously as possible. I didn't see anyone. The cars driving by didn't look suspicious so I kept walking, though I stuck to the middle of the sidewalk and avoided the gathering shadows. Dark still came early this time of year.

I burrowed my chin into my jacket and tried to look unassuming and anonymous. In the back of my mind, I worried that one of the Wolves would recognize me. That would be a very bad thing. Unsure how I knew, I was positive that I'd crossed some sort of line. *Persona non grata* didn't even come close to describing what I was to the Nightriders.

Sticking to the shadows now, I crept toward the staircase leading up to my squat. I'd climbed three steps when someone grabbed me from behind, and I knew I was in desperate trouble. Two men. They blindfolded and gagged me, tied my wrists and ankles, and one tossed me over his shoulder. I was dead. It didn't matter if these guys were Hell Dogs or Nightriders. Either would kill me.

EASY

AWARENESS TEASED MY BARE SKIN. My whiskey-soaked brain attempted to process that whispered feeling, to make sense of what was happening. My nostrils flared at the scent tiptoeing in on the breeze. I'd left the window of the office open and, as my dick swelled and my balls ached, I wished I'd closed the damn thing. That scent teased and tantalized, like phantom pains when a guy lost a limb. Honeysuckle and gunpowder—sweet and deadly. Sam.

She was back.

She had to be. I'd caught elusive hints of her scent for a couple of weeks now but nothing as strong as this. I heard voices out in the compound. Digger. Hardy. Fuckin' A. Sam was with them.

I tore through the door into the clubroom. Knocked one of the whores on her ass. Took down a brother with my shoulder, I careened through the clubroom and dashed into the kitchen. None of the old ladies were here. That was bad. Their mates didn't allow them on property when there was punishment to be dealt. Fuck. Fuck, fuck, fuck. Sam. She's all I could think about.

I smashed through the door and stumbled into the interior yard. Russki faced Digger and Hardy. Someone—no, not someone, Sam—slumped between the two of them, cut ropes dangling from her wrists. I slid to a stop and Digger shoved Sam to her knees in front of me. Her scent scorched my nose. Honeysuckle, gunpowder, and ammonia so thick I couldn't breathe.

"She's been back at least two weeks, spying on Repo's house." Digger gritted the words out through his clenched jaw.

Two weeks. She'd been around for two weeks. Or longer. Those phantom scents weren't figments of my imagination. She'd been here the whole fucking time. Hiding from me.

"She trying to snatch the kids?" Was that my voice? Fuck. I should have icicles hanging from my tongue and the scraggly beard I'd grown. With no Sam to kiss and face fuck, no need to shave.

Russski twisted his fingers in her hair and jerked her head back, baring her throat. He tugged the gag below her chin. My fingers flexed involuntarily as I reined in my wolf. He wanted to rip her to shreds, to gut her and bury his muzzle. Right after he fucked her. My dick was so hard the tip of it thrust out of the top of my jeans, wet and glistening with pre-cum.

"No," the word a whispered denial from between her lying lips. Except I didn't smell rotten apples. Ammonia, bitter and acrid, still laced the air, but beneath it I caught a hint of wet ashes, of dead roses and almonds. Regret.

Sam didn't fight when Russki jerked off the blindfold. He'd hauled her around so that her back was to me, but I knew she'd recognized my voice. All she could see, though, was the Russian at his most fierce, flanked by Hardass and Gravedigger. There was no pity in their expressions.

"If you did not come back to take the children, why are you here, Samantha Prescott?"

Her shoulders slumped even as Russki kept her facing upward by the pressure of his hand in her hair.

She didn't speak, not for a long time. My nostrils flared. Her fear was abating, to be replaced by...? I sniffed, tilting my head as I sifted through the various odors. There. Just a whiff. Damp, moldy earth. An abandoned house, musty and dank. My mother stank of that scent right before she swallowed a bottle of pills and left me alone when I was fourteen. Resignation. Sam had given up.

I looked up to find Russki and the other two Wolves watching me. The Russian's eyes were hooded. He deliberately yanked her up off the ground and shook her. Her arms and legs flailed like a limp sock monkey. "Answer me, *shlyukha*. You are my slut now, *da*?"

"I tried to leave. I meant to go back to Utah. At least until everything blew over." Sam's voice sounded subdued, with no inflection. "But I couldn't."

"You couldn't? Or wouldn't?" Hardy snarled at her.

"Couldn't. The kids. I knew they were safe, but I couldn't run out on them."

"Ah. The *deti*. Yes. So the children are the only reason." Russki dropped her, and she curled up in a ball.

"No."

"I did not hear you. What did you say to me?"

God, I'm so sorry, Easy.

I stared down at her. Sam's lips hadn't moved. I was so fucking stunned, I just stood there.

"No," she said a little louder. "They aren't the only reason. I got as far as Lawrence. Had to turn around, come back." Tears clogged her voice.

Before I could react, Hardy and Digger had her spread out on the ground, and Russki was unzipping his fucking jeans. What the hell?

"Then you must have missed me, *samka*."

Her eyes finally flicked up to mine as her tears spilled over. "No. Easy. I couldn't leave Easy."

"Do you wish him to fuck you, *samka*?"

Samka. Mate. Not his. Mine. My wolf tore through the leash I held on him and howled. The fucking Russian laughed, then threw back his head and howled with me.

"Fuck her, Easy. Fuck her here and now to claim her. But know if she crosses the Nightriders again, I will order you to slit her throat."

Still laughing, he led Digger and Hardy back through the kitchen door. I stood there, hands shoved in my pockets because they'd partially shifted into claws. My wolf wanted her, but he was wary too.

"Can you ever forgive me?"

I didn't know if I could or not. "You shredded me, Sam."

"I...I know. I'm so sorry." Her voice broke, but she sat up and curled her knees to her chest. She dropped her cheek to one knee, her face turned away.

Squatting, I touched her leg. "Look at me."

She flipped cheeks so I could see her face, but she wouldn't meet my eyes.

"Why, Sam?"

"You scared me."

"How the fuck did I scare you? I've never hit you. Never touched you in anger. But I'm tellin' you, babe. I'm about this close to losing my shit. I *want* to hurt you, but there's no way my beating you would ever compare to what you did to my heart. Everything, Sam. I gave you fucking everything I am and you pissed it away. Pissed me away. And the hell of it is? I *can't* hurt you. I'd chew off my own gawddamned hand before I did."

"Oh, God, Easy." And then she couldn't talk anymore. She was crying too hard.

I did the only thing I could. I pulled her into my arms and held her. Held her until the storm of tears stopped. Held her until the moon climbed high in the sky. Held her until she raised her face to mine, her lips finding my clenched jaw and kissing it until I relaxed. I stretched her out on the ground and lay beside her.

"Do you know what you're doing?" Sam sounded out of breath.

The stars glistened in her eyes as she stared up at me. I brushed my fingers across her lips. "I do now." Lowering my head I touched my lips to hers. Her mouth softened for me, and I sank into her. The taste of her mouth, her skin, and the texture of both, aroused, soothed, seduced. The shape of her—the athletic legs, the curvy torso, the firm breasts that just fit the palms of my hands—made me want to howl.

She tugged at our shirts—the one I wore and the one she'd stolen from me in Utah that covered her now. I helped by simply ripping the one she wore down the middle then jerking mine over my head. Flesh met flesh. She arched against me, a throaty moan teasing my senses. I burrowed deeper against her.

The night air chilled our skin, but blood heated inside me, and I could feel her skin burning with a fever. She breathed as our mouths met again, a soft sigh against my lips and our tongues danced in a long wet kiss that slipped from gentle to urgent.

Her breath hitched, and she moaned as I moved restlessly down her body, my mouth leaving trails of kisses against her hot flesh.

More. All. Everything, I thought. Then I stopped thinking.

Her cheek, her shoulders, the soft curves of them. I fed on them, then like a starving wolf, I fell on her tits, tasting, sucking, nipping until it seemed I fed on her heart as well. Shuddering, she curled closer to me, offering everything as her hands streaked over my back, taking, demanding more from me.

I did that to her, I could make her want more than she'd known there was to have. It would always be like this between us. My hands stroked her, my mouth followed. She dug her nails into the flesh of my back, trying to ride the storm of pleasure we generated.

I got free of her hands, moved lower between her legs. Fuck. Her scent exploded fireworks in my head. Her need swamped me, and I had to taste her pussy. I licked her, sucked her clit. I lapped her juices, and I wanted to shift and roll in her scent. I tongued her then used my hand. She was so wet, so hot and tight that I almost came when she squeezed around my fingers. Mine. She was fucking mine.

SAM

OH. MY. GOD. I couldn't breathe. I tried to touch Easy, but my fingers slipped off his sweat-coated skin, and his hair was too short.

I grabbed handfuls of the dirt beneath me. My body bucked, out of control, as his mouth sucked my clit and his fingers plunged in and out of my vagina. I hadn't been a virgin since I was sixteen, but holy hell, Easy made me crazy. That had to be it. I was insane. Or drugged. We were in the middle of the freaking Nightrider compound, and the stars were whirling above me like some crazy LSD dream. Dizzy, I closed my eyes, but it didn't matter. I still saw the stars swirling against my lids, and then meteors exploded inside me. I went limp, liquid, unable to move even though my hips still arched instinctively against him in a slow, sinuous rhythm.

He moved up my body, slow, kissing his way. His urgency—mine—mellowed toward tenderness. A caress, a whisper of words I couldn't quite understand, a gentle shift as he settled between my thighs, center to center.

I stroked his shoulders then ran my palms over his head, feeling the bristles of his short hair before tunneling through the longer strands on top. A part of me wished the sides of his hair were longer so I could tangle my fingers in it. I found the curve of his throat with my lips, nuzzled the pulse beating out of control. For me. I gasped when he slipped inside me, his cock stretching me almost to the point it burned. I wanted to cry because this felt so right. So perfect. I opened my eyes to find him watching me.

No one, I thought as the breath trembled in my chest, no one had ever looked at me as he did. In a way that told me I was his everything.

I rose to him, withdrew, felt him surge in to recapture me. This dance between male and female was as old as time, and as patient and pure. His rhythm stayed slow, sliding in and out as our lips met again.

I felt him say my name. "Samantha." The word hung in the air like it had been etched with a sparkler.

I wrapped my arms around him, held him close, and we found our release together, a gentle slide over the top that was full of tenderness. It felt like I was coming home. No. It didn't *feel* like I was coming home. I was home.

Chapter 17

EASY

SAM WAS IN DEEP SHIT with the Nightriders, not that I gave a good gawddamn. She was my mate, and they expected me to deal with her. The problem was the other old ladies—specifically the ones mated to Wolves. Since Sam had made friends with Sunny and Ginger to begin with, I figured those two would teach her the ropes. Yeah, that wasn't happening. Who knew Sunny would carry a grudge?

My apartment off property was about the same size as my room in the Barracks, but wasn't as clean. Necessity dictated I find a place big enough for Sam and me, plus the kids. The house needed to be close to the compound and hopefully near some of the other Nightriders with old ladies. Sam wasn't allowed in the compound unless I was with her. She figured out quick she'd better wear my patch at all times while there. She left it in my room one time, and I almost killed the motherfucker who laid hands on her. After that, she got the message loud and clear.

I'd moved her Jeep from the spot where she'd hidden it, surprised as hell it hadn't been stolen or stripped. Then I saw the graffiti on the wall. One of the brothers had marked the derelict building as Nightrider territory. There wasn't a jerkwad in three counties stupid enough to steal something from there now. I parked the Jeep at my apartment, and made her ride on my Harley whenever we went out. It pissed her off, but I got turned on by having her right behind me. Once the weather got warm enough, I was gonna fuck Sam on my bike, driving down the road full throttle. My dick jumped to attention every time I pictured it.

The Blood Moon was just over two weeks away. None of us were stupid enough—or strong enough—to challenge Russki. He was uptight though, halfway expecting one of the local presidents to challenge for national leadership. We'd be burying the body if one did. No one could take the Russian.

Hollywood, that asshole, decided we needed to party before all the shit went down. He cleared it with the officers and proceeded to invite all the area chapters and every girl on his call list.

"Gotta have lots of pussy on hand, right?"

Digger, Hardy, Wizard, and all the unattached brothers agreed. Me? I had all the pussy I ever wanted. All I had to do was look at Sam, and she'd get wet. But first things first. A place to live then the party. All the old ladies were in charge of food. Except the meat. Repo, Radar, and Digger were the master grillers. We had a big ass grill out back. They'd smoked ribs, roasts, even a fucking half steer one time. Radar swore he was gonna do a pig like at a luau or something.

The women shut Sam out of things. Her feelings were hurt, but it's not like she wasn't at fault and deserved some of it. Calling Repo a monster to his mate's face? That was pretty damn stupid. I was getting regular pussy, and my wolf was doing his one-for-the-team thing so we'd forgiven her for ripping my heart out and stomping on it. The old ladies had a soft spot in their hearts for me, and they weren't as quick to forgive.

A week before the party, I lucked out and found a place. I put in an offer, made the down-payment, and closed on it without talking to Sam. I figured if she could squat in an abandoned building with nothing but a sleeping bag, she could live in this house. It had five bedrooms, a big garage, and the Realtor kept bragging about the kitchen and bathroom remodels. Besides, we could take possession immediately. Good thing Sam liked it.

I sent her off to shop for furniture with instructions not to buy anything that couldn't be delivered immediately. I called in reinforcements, and by the time she got back, all my stuff from the apartment had been moved in. I have a crazy-ass big custom bed. It took six of us to wrangle that bitch into the downstairs master bedroom.

By the day of the party, we'd settled in with the kids. They were excited about going. I'd already explained to Sam that for the first part of the night, there'd be a lot of kids around because it was family time. There might not be many Wolf pups around, but some of the human brothers bred like rabbits. Sam sulked because staying home with the kids was her excuse to duck out of the party.

"Babe, ya gotta get over this shit."

"Me? I've done everything I can to make up with them. They ignore me, or cut me off and walk away. You have no idea what it's like!"

She had me there. I didn't understand women and the fucking games they played with each other. If you pissed off another Nightrider, punches were thrown then you sat down with the asshole and shared a cold beer. There was none of this holding onto grudges and hurt feelings and crap.

"You're right."

Sam stared at me, her mouth hanging open about half an inch. I leaned over and kissed her. "Either they get over it or they don't, baby." I tugged her against my chest. "They may never be your friends, but they respect the patch. Just help out even if they ignore you. Once things wind down with the kids, you can leave."

"What about you?"

"I'm an officer, Sam. I gotta stay."

"Oh."

Damn. I fucking hated when she sounded all small and wounded like that. I kissed the top of her head and squeezed her tighter. "It'll be okay. We're expecting close to three hundred people. You'll find someone there to hang out with."

SAM

TONIGHT WOULD BE an unmitigated disaster. I could almost see the black cloud hanging over my head. I'd spent days in the kitchen—which was freaking fantastic for cooking in. How Easy got so lucky with this house, I'll never know. I couldn't have picked out a better place. I hadn't cooked in ages, but with this kitchen, I intended to make up for lost time. I baked pies—deep dish apple, cherry, key lime, chocolate meringue, coconut cream. I made cakes—chocolate, red velvet, angel food. I made cookies—double chunk chocolate with pecans, sugar, snickerdoodles, oatmeal raisin, peanut butter.

Friggin' Easy and Jonah thought they'd died and gone to heaven. Noni just wanted her Nilla Wafers. I was determined to find a recipe for those suckers. I mean, it wasn't like I had anything else to do. I didn't want to get a job until the kids were settled, and it's not like the other old ladies—and I *still* hated that term, but refused to rock the boat any more than I had already—were knocking on the door to spend time with me.

Easy got a call from Radar, who ran the bail bond company, and took off with a half-assed promise that he'd see me later at the clubhouse. Whoopee. I loaded up all the desserts and the kids in the Jeep and headed over in the middle of the afternoon. Maybe I could sneak in, drop off this stuff, and high-tail it out of there. I was damn tired of the catty bitches. I'd done everything I could think of to apologize. None of them would give me the time of day and frankly, treated me like one of the club whores, despite what Easy believed.

When I drove up to the gate, I figured to get hassled since Easy wasn't with us. Instead, Hollywood stuck his head in the window and took a big ol' sniff.

"Mmmm. You smell like my momma's house the day before Christmas. Gimme a cookie and I'll help you unload."

"Deal."

Maybe things were getting better. Or maybe I just had good bribes. If all it took was a bakery load of desserts to win these guys over, then I'd bake every freaking day of the week. Hollywood jumped up on the hood of the Jeep to ride around back. I pulled up not far from the door, thinking to off load and then move the Jeep.

Repo, Radar, and Gravedigger were lording over the biggest grill setup I'd ever seen. It was fifteen feet long, had a metal chimney at one end, and about six different lids. The aroma wafting from it was divine. A handful of kids played on the fortified swing set built for Jonah and Noni. At my nod, they took off to join the others. At least Easy hadn't lied. There were other kids here.

I handed Hollywood the boxes of cookies, and I grabbed two of the pies. Sunny was in charge of the kitchen, but smiled as soon as Hollywood asked where to put desserts. "That table back there, hon. Whatcha' got?"

He shrugged. "No clue. Easy's woman brought 'em." He stepped sideways, leaving me standing there, exposed.

Sunny glared, but didn't say anything. Some women I'd never seen before were present so she was probably keeping our club business in-house. We sure wouldn't want the neighbors to hear us squabbling, now would we?

"Those are cookies." I ran down the list. "This is a deep dish apple pie, and I think this one is the chocolate meringue. I have more pies and three cakes out in the Jeep."

"Damn, girl. Did you buy out a bakery?" A brassy redhead sauntered up. "I'm Marie, Deadhead's old lady. He's president of the Topeka chapter."

"Oh, hi. I'm Sam. I'm Easy's...old lady." I didn't mean to stumble over the words. I'd been practicing saying them all week. "Old lady" was a whole lot better than "Easy's property." Sunny snorted and rolled her eyes before giving me her back. "And no, these aren't store bought. I've been baking all week."

With Marie's help, we got the goodies unloaded, and I moved the Jeep, under Hollywood's direction, to the designated parking area. With a reminder to Jonah to look after his little sister, I squared my shoulders and marched back into the kitchen. To hell with Sunny and Ginger and anyone else who thought I was pond scum. I'd do my part despite them.

I ended up supervising the club whores on cleaning detail. First, they had to scrub all the unassigned bedrooms and bathrooms in the Barracks. We even put fresh sheets on the beds. I guess some of the out-of-town bikers would be sleeping here. Or getting fucked if the conversation swirling around me was any indication. By the time I wrangled them into doing a thorough job with the clubroom and bar, I was hot, sweaty, and out of sorts. I needed to go home and clean up. I thought about using the bathroom in Easy's room, but I no longer kept clothes here. Once we had possession of the house, I moved every scrap of my stuff. I couldn't put the clubhouse in my rearview mirror fast enough.

Making a mental note to pack a go-bag to leave in Easy's room in case of emergency, I headed back to the kitchen. I didn't make the mistake of reaching for a can of Diet Coke in the fridge. I'd been told bluntly that unless I stocked my own, I could just drink water from the tap. That's what I did. I grabbed a plastic glass advertising a local restaurant and filled it from the sink faucet. The old ladies, including about ten more I'd never seen before, were gathered around the huge table. Everyone ignored me so Sunny and Ginger must have filled them in on my lack of status.

I rolled my shoulders in an attempt to ignore the hurt. I didn't want to be one of them anyway. Sneaking home to clean up and change would mean corralling Jonah and Noni. They wouldn't be happy. This was the first time they'd had other kids to play with since their mom was killed. I couldn't do it to them.

The clubroom was full and getting fuller as more people arrived. Rowdy, loud, the bikers were already drinking. Girls, some I'd never seen before, filtered in and sized up the men, receiving heated looks in return. I scuttled out the front door and found a shady nook tucked back where I could watch the activity at the front gate. Six Nightriders were on duty, including two fully patched-in members. The guy called Wizard was one of them. I wasn't positive, but I got the Wolf vibe from him, just like I did Hollywood.

Members brought their vehicles through the gates, men on bikes sometimes followed by women in cars. Sort of hard to transport food on a motorcycle. Non-members—the idiot kids who thought they wanted to grow up to be Nightriders, and the girls out for a thrill with a big, bad biker had to park outside the fence, along the road. I watched for Easy in vain.

The sun was setting when Hollywood reappeared. "C'mon, hon. The party's around back."

"I'm waiting for Easy."

He pulled me away from the wall where I'd plastered my back, turned me around, and tapped the patch on my jacket. "Says here PROPERTY OF EASY. You'll be safe enough."

How did I explain it wasn't the brothers I

was worried about, but their women? Before I opened my mouth, he looped an arm around my neck and walked me the long way around the building. It made me wonder what was happening inside the clubroom. I definitely needed to keep the kids out of there.

Tables, chairs, and benches had miraculously appeared in the rough square created by the main building, the Barracks, and the garage. Dang. I was probably in trouble with the old ladies again for not being there to fetch and carry.

Hollywood hip-bumped me, as if he'd read my mind. "We big strong men do the set up and tear down and tend the meat. But the old ladies are starting to bring food out. You need to help with that."

And then it occurred to me. Easy wasn't coming, and he'd asked Hollywood to look after me. I should be pissed, but a sense of relief settled over me. Still, I needed to confirm my suspicions. "Easy won't be here, will he?"

"Sorry, babe. The Russian sent him over to Chasin' Tail to handle things tonight. Shit happens when a brother gets bumped to the bottom of the totem pole. He's on the night shift's garbage detail until Russki decides Easy's paid his penance. Besides, with most of us here in the compound, civilian assholes might get the idea they can cause problems."

Easy knew I wouldn't have come without him. I heard the squeal of children's laughter, and my gaze immediately landed on Jonah and Noni. They were both playing with kids their own ages. And having a ball. That's why Easy had lied by omission to me. Pissed me off that he'd lie, and we would have a very heated discussion about his propensity to do so, but I couldn't deny the kids this chance to be normal for awhile.

I ducked from under Hollywood's arm. "Thanks. Guess it's time to get back to work."

Trudging across the grass, I avoided direct contact with anyone and slipped through the kitchen door. I grabbed dishes from the table and headed back out to put them on the buffet tables. I laughed. Buffet and biker were not two terms that should go together. Once the food was out, the Russian stood in the middle of the square, backed by his officers—minus Easy—and seven other men, all wearing chapter president patches. Old ladies scrambled to grab kids and shush them.

The Russian's voice, tinted with his accent, rang in the air. "Welcome, brothers. Nightriders forever. Forever Nightriders." He raised his beer bottle and more than three hundred voices repeated the mantra. So much for long, boring speeches.

A bonfire flared to life and the women who

had children guided them to the food table, filling their plates and getting them settled at a table set aside just for them. Jonah fended for himself while I shepherded Noni through the line. Once they found places to sit, I headed to the dessert table then my Jeep. Jonah loved my deep dish apple pie and Noni would want her box of Nillas. I snagged their desserts, made sure Noni was eating without help, and drifted off to hide in the shadows.

Alone. I'd better get used to it. Without Easy beside me, I felt lost and out of sorts. I didn't fit in here. Never would. But Easy was a Nightrider, and I was more than his old lady. I was his mate. He was so firmly lodged in my heart I'd never get him out. And didn't want to. Granted, the sex was abso-freaking-amazing, but there was more between us. I had a bone-deep need for him. And he was firmly entrenched in the Nightriders. I couldn't separate those halves of him. I wouldn't. So for him, and for the kids to be safe, I'd accept being the outsider. Being ostracized was a small price to pay. And, once we were away from these walls, nothing else mattered. Just Easy. Just...us.

EIGHTEEN

SAM

THE FAMILY PART of this shindig wound down as kids got sleepy. The adult entertainment portion ramped up. Couples filtered into the shadows, and the clubroom had been posted off limits to minors. I'd held out hope that Hollywood was wrong and Easy would appear after all. He hadn't, and Noni was all but asleep on my lap.

I struggled to stand up with her. When had the little dickens gotten so big? Hollywood appeared out of the dark, Jonah in tow. He took Noni from me and carried her to my Jeep. With the baby in her car seat and Jonah buckled in, I turned to Hollywood.

"Thanks for your help tonight. I'll be back in the morning to help clean up."

"Wait for me at the gate, hon. I'll grab my bike and follow you home."

"That's not necessary. Really. We live close, and I'm used to taking care of myself." I glanced over his shoulder. A blonde with big boobs watched us, and she was not happy that Hollywood was paying attention to me.

"Besides, I think you have other plans for the night." I gave him a wink-wink-nudge-nudge with my elbow. "Go get laid, Hollywood."

A grin split his face. "Oh, fuck yeah." He hissed out a breath and ducked his head to check on the kids. Noni was already asleep, and Jonah was engrossed in some video game on my smart phone. "Sorry."

I waved away his language slip in front of the kids. "It's not like Easy doesn't do it all the time. Have fun."

Still, he hesitated. "Are you sure?"

"Positive."

The prospects opened the gate for us, and I drove through, with a big sigh of relief. I'd survived. It wasn't very late, only about eleven, but the streets seemed deserted. Hair prickled on my arms, and I started paying closer attention to my surroundings. The Nightriders' compound sat on the edge of an industrial area, not too far from a major highway. The lights of a convenience store glimmered up ahead, and I realized how dark this area actually was.

Crossing an intersection with no street lights, I caught movement out of the corner of my eye. There was a car parked midway down the side street. And bikes. I got a really bad feeling. I circled through the store's parking lot and headed back. This was probably one of the stupidest things I'd ever done, especially since the kids were with me, but I had to check out the situation. Taking a couple of turns, I got on the cross street so I could use my headlights to see.

I'd seen a similar car parked not far from mine. Teri. Toni. Something like that. She lived with a Nightrider named Sandhog. Did she have car trouble or something? One of the guys surrounding her turned around to stare at me just as I got a good look at the back patch on another. Hell Dogs.

"Jonah, call Easy. Tell him we need help right now. Near that convenience store on Parris and a Hundred and Fortieth."

"Aunt Sam? What's wrong?"

"Trouble, Jojo. Stay out of sight and call Easy." I dug under my seat before I remembered Easy had taken all the weapons out. I didn't have my pistol. I didn't have my knife. Damn, damn, damn.

One of the Hell Dogs shielded his eyes from the glare of my lights and started walking toward us. I flicked on my brights, threw the transmission in reverse, and goosed the accelerator. When I hit the next intersection, I shifted into the drive and whipped the Jeep around the corner, headed away. But I wasn't leaving. I couldn't leave Teri alone with them. God only knew what they'd do to her. She was a quiet girl, a little shy, but sweet and more than willing to help out wherever she was needed. A part of my brain heard Jonah leave a desperate message.

"He didn't answer, Aunt Sam. What do I do now?"

I racked my brain for numbers. A month and a half ago, I would have just called 9-1-1 but now? Maybe I'd fallen too deeply into the rabbit hole of MC existence, but I knew they wouldn't want the cops involved. It was up to me to get Teri out of there.

"Sunny. Find Sunny's number in my phone. Call her. Tell her Teri is in trouble, that Hell Dogs have her."

I pulled into a dark parking lot not far from the store. "Stay in the Jeep, Jonah. And keep the doors locked. Don't open them for anyone but me, Easy, or one of the Nightriders you know. Understood?"

He nodded mutely then returned his attention to my phone. I got out, rummaged around until I found the crowbar in my emergency kit. It would have to do for a weapon. As I closed the hatch, I heard Jojo talking.

"Aunt Sunny? Aunt Sunny? Please. We need you. We need Easy and Uncle Repo and everyone. Bad trouble, Aunt Sunny. Aunt Sam says it's Hell Dogs, and they have Teri. Aunt Sunny? Are you there?"

I didn't have time to find out if she'd answered. It didn't occur to me that she might ignore the call because it came from my phone. All I knew was Teri needed help, and I was the only one available.

EASY

THREE DRUNKEN BRAWLS. A dancer who got stiffed on her private party fee. A shortage of Jack Daniels. A typical Saturday night at Chasin' Tail. I knew why I got the shit detail. Russki wanted to cut Sam's support out from under her to see how she handled the party without me. Pissed me off, but who was I to argue. I couldn't fix things for her. She had to do it herself. That was just a fact of MC life.

The phone in my back pocket buzzed. I checked caller ID. Sam. Probably calling to say she and the kids were home. Hollywood would have followed them so it was all good. Two guys pushed back from the bar and stood nose-to-nose. Time to break up another fucking fight.

Ten minutes later, my wolf was ready to chew his way out of my gut. Something was wrong. Bad wrong. Sam. I jerked the phone out my pocket. She'd left a message—five in fact. It wasn't her voice when I hit play on the last one.

"Dad! Dad, you gotta come quick. Hell Dogs. They've got Aunt Sam. Nobody's answering their phones. Nobody's coming to help. Please, daddy. Where are you?"

Dad? Jonah called me dad, but I didn't have time to consider the implication. Sam was in trouble. Where the fuck was Hollywood? I grabbed the prospect working the front door. "Call for backup. There's shit going down. I gotta go."

On the way to my bike, I listened to the rest of the messages. Sam and the kids weren't far from the compound. I called Sam's phone, got a busy signal. Fuck. I called Repo. No answer. I called Digger. No answer. I called fucking Hollywood.

"Fuck off, Easy. She went home forty-five minutes ago. She's fine, and I'm fucking a sexy blonde." He cut the call off.

I planned to cut off his balls for this. I dialed the Russian. He answered on the first ring. I could hear the sounds of sex in the background. Some club whore was probably on her knees sucking him off. I didn't fucking care.

"Jonah fucking called me. Sam and the kids are in trouble with Hell Dogs. There was something about Sandhog's old lady, too. The store at Parris and One-forty. If anything happens to her, to them, I'm going fucking rogue, you bastard." I hung up before he said anything and jammed the phone in my pocket.

I was probably doing a hundred when I

imagined Sam's voice in my head.

Easy? Easy where are you? Need you. Trouble. So much trouble.

"I'm comin', baby. Hang on. Just hang the fuck on."

I set a new land speed record getting from Chasin' Tail to that gawddamned store. Sam's Jeep was parked nearby. Wizard and two prospects stood next to it. Wiz flashed a thumbs up as I drove by. The kids were okay. Down the block, the street was clogged with choppers. My kickstand barely touched pavement before I was off and running.

Sam stood on the sidewalk by herself, her arms wrapped across her chest. There was blood on her face, and she looked so brittle that one wrong word might shatter her. Sandhog was there, cuddling his old lady. Teri cried softly, her face buried in Hog's chest. Russki, Digger, Hardy, and Hollywood stood over a body. My wolf lost his shit. Three steps and I punched Hollywood in the face.

"You fucking dickwad." I hauled him up and hit him again before Digger and Hardy pulled me off.

"Easy. Do not do something you will regret." Russki's threat wasn't loud, but it was damned effective.

"Too busy fucking some bitch to take care of my mate. That's all I asked of you, *bro*." Guilt welled up inside. I'd ignored her call, too, but fuckin' A, I was working, doing what my president and Alpha told me to do, taking care of club business. And did the fucking club take care of my business? Hell no.

"Easy." Russki again, only this time, the ice in his voice brought me to heel.

I backed away, turned to Sam. She just stood there, staring at me. "Sam?"

"Don't touch me."

Ah, fuck. The hurt on her face twisted in my gut. Betrayed. She felt betrayed. By everyone, but especially me.

"What happened?"

"We were headed home. I told Hollywood to stay at the compound. I passed this street, saw something. Circled around. Teri was surrounded by four Hell Dogs. I—Jonah tried to call you. Tried to call Sunny." Her breath hitched. "Nobody answered."

I growled at that. This petty revenge shit had gone fucking far enough. It had almost cost me Sam and the kids.

"I couldn't leave Teri. I had to help."

Fuck. I'd taken all the weapons out of her Jeep, at the Russian's command. I cleared my throat and glanced at the Hell Dog bleeding all over the asphalt. "Who did that?"

"Me."

"How?" Not that I didn't believe her, but the more I got Sam to talk, the less brittle she seemed.

"He thought he could take me. I hit him in the gut with that." She pointed to a bloody crow bar next to the body. "When he doubled over, I put my knee in his face, and then I kicked him in the nuts."

Forcing a grin, I swiped a finger across her arm. "You know, that makes me kinda hot."

She raised her eyes to meet mine. Fuck. They looked bruised, broken. "One of them will probably have a broken wrist. He had a knife. I hit him. He didn't fight after that. The other two let go of Teri. I told her to run, but she was too scared."

A shudder ran through her, and I reached out, but she stepped backwards, away from me, shaking her head. "One of them hit Teri, and she went down. They both came for me. I fought, but they got the crow bar. Then I heard motorcycles. So did they. They took off."

"God, baby. I'm sorry." I couldn't stand it any longer. My wolf was snapping and whining. We needed to hold her, pet her, know that she really was okay. I crowded her up against the building, gathered her into my arms, and just held her. She struggled against me, and then sagged when the fight went out of her.

Behind me, I heard the Russian talking to Repo.

"I'll check her phone, Russki, and talk to

her." Repo sounded contrite, but pissed. Probably at Sam for implicating Sunny.

"No. I will check her phone. Tell her to come here. Now."

Damn. The Russian didn't get involved in our personal lives as a rule. But if an old lady or one of the club whores threatened the security of the MC, all bets were off. Repo moved off to speak quietly into his phone.

Five minutes later, Sunny pulled up in her Charger. She did not look happy. "What the hell, Repo?" She thrust her phone at him, and then got a look at Sam. Her eyes widened, and a little moan escaped when she saw Teri.

Repo hit the speaker button and played back the messages from Jonah. His desperation grew more apparent with each phone call. The kid must have called me, called Sunny, and then alternated between us until help arrived.

Sunny, her face stricken, stared at her mate. "I didn't know. I just thought...I don't know what I thought. If I'd known it was Jonah, that the kids were in trouble—"

"Fuck you, Sunny." I growled at the woman, and Repo's hackles came up. "It's fine if Sam is in trouble? So you wouldn't do jack shit to help *her*? She's my gawddamn mate, Sunny. That should fucking mean something."

"She's not good enough for you, Easy! She

191

called you a damn monster. She called all of you monsters!"

Russki stepped between us. "This is a discussion for later." He raised his voice. "Sandhog, take Teri home. If she needs anything...if *you* need anything, call."

No one said a word until the two humans vacated the area. Once they were clear, Russki stepped back. He leaned a hip against Sunny's car. "How old were you, Sunny, when you saw your first Wolf?"

She looked confused for a minute and frowned. "I don't remember. My dad was a Wolf."

"Yes. You grew up knowing us, knowing what we are, what we do." He pointed toward Sam. She'd slid down to squat on the cracked sidewalk, leaning against the rough brick wall at her back. "Samantha saw her first not even two months ago when the man she loved shifted from wolf to man with blood on his mouth from ripping out the throat of a Hell Dog."

"But she ran away." Sunny spat the words.

My fingers itched to touch Sam, but I stared Sunny down instead. "She came back." Movement caught my attention. Sam had pushed to her feet and was walking toward me.

"It doesn't matter. What's done is done. Teri is safe. My kids are safe." She glared at the Russian. "I will be carrying from now on. I don't give a damn what you say about it." She took several more steps before she glanced back at Sunny. "Fuck you and the high horse you rode in on, Sunny. I don't need your friendship. In fact, I don't need a damn thing from you. From any of you. Stay away from my kids. Stay away from me."

Sam's eyes flicked to me. "I'm leaving, Easy. Do whatever shit you have to do then come home to me."

With that, she marched away, head held high. I'd never been so proud of anyone in my fucking life. Stunned silence rushed in to fill the void left by her exit. Long moments later, Hollywood cleared his throat. He'd gotten to his feet and stood nearby, his head lowered in submission.

"I'd like to go with her. I'll take Wiz and two prospects. We'll make sure she gets home and stays safe until you get there, Easy."

I glanced at Russki. A scant dip of his chin answered my unasked question. "Thanks."

And that was the end of it. Hollywood knew he'd fucked up. It didn't matter that Sam told him it was okay. He didn't take orders from her. He took orders from me and the other officers. He'd take his punishment, just like I had, and he understood that if something had happened to Sam or the kids, I would have killed him. Men's relationships were easy. Women? Not so much.

RUSSKI

WOMEN. They were good for one thing only but these moonstruck Wolves? They forgot that. Dealing with them made my head hurt. I had no mate. Would never have one for this very reason.

I stared at the bloody aftermath of the attack on Teri. Body disposal used to be simple. I once considered buying a pig farm for that very reason. In my home country, this was not an issue. Only in America, with its honest cops, forensic scientists, and prudish sensibilities. I watched Digger and Easy roll the Hell Dog formally known as Lumpy into a plastic tarp and slap Velcro straps around it. Sam left him breathing. By the time we finished questioning him, he no longer was. He gave us every bit of information he had, despite his fear of the one he called Fallen Angel. This was someone new, someone who had taken over the Hell Dogs with blood and death.

"Nothing with a zipper?"

Finishing the last strap, Hardy explained. "Asshole's too fat to stuff in a standard duffel bag, boss. We woulda had t'cut 'im up. Gets messy."

Gravedigger came by his name honestly. He snorted and offered me a sardonic smile.

"Seems the president of the MC said to get our fuckin' asses back here ASAP. We grabbed what we had."

I released an exaggerated sigh. "I do miss the old days."

My enforcer's guffaw rang so loud the murder of crows gathered on the fence beside us erupted into the dawn sky. "Shit, Russki. In the old days, we woulda just shifted and ate the motherfucker."

"Ah, this is true, but we have a message to deliver, yes?"

"Damn straight," Easy growled. He no longer resembled his name. These last months had hardened the once easy-going Wolf. He had family now, beyond the brotherhood of Nightriders. "They touch any of our women again, we'll burn the fuckers alive."

I offered a smile too cold to reach the darkness in my soul. "Yes. We will consign them all to the fires of Hell, but first, we find the one called Fallen Angel. We will see what this devil does against Wolves. Time for a social call."

NINETEEN

SAM

I STILL DIDN'T LIKE hanging around the Nightrider clubhouse but Easy asked me to come tonight. Now, standing outside, I wished I'd stayed home. The testosterone was so thick I had trouble breathing, and every hair on my body stood straight up in warning. I glanced at the other women and knew immediately their reactions were the same as mine. Two strange men stood just inside the gate completely surrounded by Nightriders. Neither of them wore cuts, but the Harleys they rode were parked on the other side of the fence.

Nearly a week had passed since that sorry excuse for a party, and the Nightriders acted like they were at war. Sunny, Ginger, and I had come to an uneasy truce. Teri was like my new best friend. She was a sweet kid, and I was glad her near-kidnapping hadn't traumatized her.

Two of the prospects attempted to herd us back inside. That so wasn't happening. The newcomers fascinated me. Raw power rolled off both men, otherworldly power like that of Easy. Wolves. They had to be. I glanced at Sunny. She'd gone white.

I almost nudged her with my elbow when I muttered, "What?"

"Blood Moon."

Blood moon? What the heck did that mean? Before I could ask, the two men started walking toward the door. And toward us, since we were bottlenecked at the front entrance. The prospects panicked. One of them grabbed Sunny, picked her up, and carried her inside. I thought Repo was going to come unglued. His expression turned all kinds of scary as he charged. I would not want to be the kid who snatched her up. The other prospect turned sheet white and gurgled while he made shooing motions with his hands. I grabbed Teri and one of the whores and urged them inside. Ginger herded the rest of the women.

Easy appeared behind me. "Get the kids off the swings and go to my room, Sam. Now. Hollywood will go with you."

Oh hell to the no. I didn't stop to argue in the foyer, but once we were in the clubroom, I corralled the other women back behind the pool table. The prospect who'd touched Sunny was unconscious on the floor, bleeding. I couldn't tell who was more pissed, Repo or the Russian. Sunny wasn't exactly happy either.

Something was definitely in the air tonight. All the Wolves had gotten progressively aggressive as this week wore on and the moon waxed toward full.

Hollywood ducked out through the kitchen. He'd keep Jonah and Noni safe until Easy and I could get there.

The Nightriders fanned out while the Russian, Digger, Hardy, and Easy escorted the new guys to the bar. Easy went behind it, grabbed a bottle and two shot glasses. He poured whiskey into the glasses and waited. I studied the two men. The one who radiated the most power looked bald, but I realized with the better light inside that his brown hair had been buzzed. Square jawed, broad-shouldered, he looked like he should be the model on a military recruiting poster: Only Bad-asses Need Enlist. The second guy's hair was almost as short, and he was serious eye candy. He seemed...lighter, like he laughed more often. There were crinkles at the corners of his eyes, and his full bottom lip pouted over the cleft in his chin.

The hair on my arms prickled, and I glanced at Easy. He was growling at me, soundlessly, but I could feel his anger all the way across the room. What? I couldn't window shop? He and I really needed to have a serious discussion about establishing the rules of our relationship. Eye Candy snagged the bottle from Easy's hand, which earned him a snarl. The dude sniffed, swirled the liquid inside, sniffed again, and then took a swig straight from the bottle. He swished it in his mouth like wine snobs do with a good Bordeaux. When he swallowed, he nodded to his partner. Only then did Soldier Man and the Russian pick up the glasses and knock back the shots.

What? Were they afraid the stuff had been poisoned? That wasn't the Nightriders' style. If they wanted to take you out, they just ripped out your throat or shot you full of bullet holes. Of course, looking at the newcomers, there would be some serious blood loss on both sides.

"We go to church now," the Russian decreed.

The strangers turned and Soldier Man's eyes narrowed. The power in the room ramped up again. Even the club whores felt it. I smoothed down the hair on my arms. He strode toward the pool table, and all of us scrambled to get out of the way. The Nightriders moved fast and presented a solid wall of MC strength for us to hide behind.

Stopping at the table, Soldier Man looked up at the pelt on the wall and turned his head to give the Russian a long, appraising look. "This your work?"

"Yes."

"Huh. Impressive."

Sunny let out a long breath, and I glanced at her. I so wanted the whole story of what was going down. I lowered my brows in question, but got only a brief shake of her head. Then she touched my arm, and her fingers were trembling. Dang. Evidently, things were headed from bad to worse, and I was out of the loop. Then again, this was the first time since the fiasco with the Hell Dogs that Sunny had interacted with me at all.

The Russian led the way, followed by the guests, while Digger, Hardy, Repo, Radar, and Easy walked right behind them. The rest of the Nightriders filed in after. The heavy wooden doors slammed shut, and we heard the locks turn. Only then did Sunny really take a breath.

"Holy cannoli," I muttered after taking my own deep breath. "Who *are* those guys?"

Sunny tugged my arm, and we moved away from the club whores, headed to the kitchen. Ginger followed us. We were the only Wolf mates on the premises. Teri and the other old ladies stayed out in the clubroom. The whores almost ran for the bar to start drinking. Once we had beers and sat down at the kitchen table, I glanced at Sunny.

"Will you talk to me?" We still had a long way to go to mend our friendship. I wasn't sure I'd ever be able to trust her, but I was willing to extend the olive branch if she was.

Sunny shrugged one shoulder and stared at my chin before flicking her gaze up to meet mine before dropping it again. "I'm sorry, Sam. Club comes first. Always. I forgot that."

This was as close to an apology as I'd get. It was a first step. "So who are those guys? What the hell is a blood moon? And what's the deal with that damn wolf pelt?"

After swigging about half the beer in her bottle, Sunny gave a delicate shudder. "I'm going to kill Easy for not filling you in completely when he claimed you."

That got my dander up. Easy told me the old ladies were supposed to fill in the blanks where the MC and Wolves were concerned. When I opened my mouth to make that clear, Sunny held up her hand.

"Don't get pissed. I'll explain what I can, but you really need to talk to Easy after church is over." She downed the rest of her beer, tossed the bottle over her shoulder, and it landed with a satisfying clink in the industrial-sized plastic trashcan. "The Blood Moon, and it's a thing, but not necessarily that whole eclipse phenomena thing, though it somehow figures into it. Which won't make much sense. Anyway, you know that—" She snapped her mouth shut and leaned back in her chair so she could see where the club whores and the other old ladies were out in the other room. Positive they couldn't overhear, she still leaned closer and motioned me to meet her halfway.

"You know the MC is set up sort of like a wolf pack and why, right?" I nodded and she continued. "There are always alphas around who want to challenge *the* Alpha, capital A. Way back whenever, rules were put into place to govern the fights for supremacy. An Alpha can only be challenged on the Blood Moon. Again, capital B, capital M."

Her explanation made sense in a weird, Dungeons and Dragons way. "Okay. So why is everyone all freaked out about these two guys showing up?"

"The wolf pelt. On the wall."

Ginger pushed back from the table and went to the fridge to grab another beer for Sunny. She didn't guzzle this time, but still took a big swig. "His name was Brick McIntire. He was the national president before the Russian showed up."

I freaked. Not just a little, but a lot. All but falling out of my chair, I jumped up and backed away. "What the fuck? That wolf pelt is..." I swallowed the bile threatening to choke me. "Was a *man*?" My voice squeaked on the last word.

Sunny nodded, her eyes as big as half dollars. "Sit, Sam."

I did as she ordered, though I collapsed

more than sat.

"Brick was a strong Alpha, and he was a royal bastard." She glanced over at Ginger. "You need to hear this too, hon." Another swig, a deep breath, and Sunny launched into the story.

"Y'all just listen, 'kay? The story is crazy convoluted so wait 'til I'm done to interrupt. When the Russian showed up to challenge Brick, he was by himself. He had no chapter to back his play, not even a second. He just walked in on the night of the Blood Moon and issued the challenge. Alphas fight in their wolf forms for dominance. The Russian changed lightning fast and caught Brick with his pants down—figuratively, not literally. The start of a dominance fight is very ritualized. The Wolves strip, and wait for some sign before they shift. Nobody had challenged Brick in...well...a long time. And that one time wasn't exactly a *challenge*."

She held up her finger when I opened my mouth. I snapped it shut, and she continued.

"When the signal was given, the Russian shifted wicked fast, and he attacked ferociously. The fight lasted a long time, and there was blood everywhere. All the non-Wolves had been sent off before the challenge started. That's another rule. Only the inner cadre witnesses it, and that's because they're always Wolves. The regular members don't know what the guys are, and if they happen to find out, they disappear. You follow?" I nodded again and felt like a freaking bobblehead. "The Russian eventually ripped out Brick's throat, and Brick shifted back to human as Wolves do when they're badly injured, or dying."

Sunny's hand shook when she picked up the beer bottle and took a long drink. "Brick was dying. The Russian shifted and just stood there for a minute. Then he forced Brick to change back into a wolf."

My eyebrows climbed to the top of my forehead. "What the hell?"

"Yeah. The Russian is such a strong Alpha he could force Brick back into wolf form." Her skin paled, and she swallowed a few times. "And then he skinned Brick." A shudder ran the length of her body. "Wolves can take massive damage and heal. It isn't spontaneous like in werewolf movies, but I've seen a Wolf with his throat torn out come back from it and live a normal life. But the Russian—" Another gulp. "He's so powerful, he made Brick shift, skinned him while he was still alive, and left him there to bleed out from the injuries. That's why the pelt is on the wall."

I gulped my own beer. What the hell kind of nightmare had I fallen into here?

"Repo's only seen one other Wolf able to do

what the Russian did. Brick was a nasty son of a bitch, and he liked to use his old lady for a punching bag. One day, this guy shows up. It wasn't a Blood Moon, but he challenged Brick anyway. Brick changed. The guy just stood there. And then Brick was human again. Every time Brick tried to shift, the guy forced him back into his human skin. Over and over. And then the guy beat the holy crap out of Brick with his fists. I mean, that man broke almost every bone in Brick's body. He had a punctured lung. Kidney damage. Hardy fixed him up as much as he could, but they had to call in a real doctor. Doc Carson removed part of Brick's liver. Anyway, I'm getting ahead of myself. In the end, the guy spit on Brick, kicked him in the head, and said, 'That's for her. You ever touch her again, I'll be back to kill you, old man.' We weren't sure Brick was going to survive."

"Jeez." I drank again and drew condensation circles on the wooden table top with the bottom of the bottle. "What happened to Brick's old lady?"

"She stayed low key after that, and we never noticed bruises on her again. Then, when the Russian took down Brick, things got a little screwy. As the former Alpha's mate, she had to offer herself to the new Alpha, since he was unmated. The Russian turned her down. She...sort of committed suicide.

Walked in front of a bus a couple of weeks after the Blood Moon challenge."

Wait. The Alpha's mate had to offer herself to the winner? That was all kinds of screwed up, but before I could comment, Sunny's next sentence sent chills down my spine.

"The Alpha who arrived tonight? He's Brick's son."

Well...hell. The light bulb clicked on. "And he's the one?"

Sunny's eyes had gotten even bigger. She wet her lips and nodded. I didn't have to read the writing on the wall to figure this out. They believed Brick McIntire's son had returned to challenge for club leadership.

EASY

I'D BEEN A GREEN KID, hoping to be accepted as a prospect when Ian McIntire made his first visit to the Nightriders. We all knew he was Brick's offspring. They looked too damn much alike not to be sire and pup. Except *pup* didn't describe the younger McIntire. He was some Special Forces badass, and he was pissed that Brick hurt his mother. He damn sure put the fear of the gods into Brick that day. Thing was, it wasn't a Blood Moon challenge, and the guy just walked away after taking the Alpha down.

By the time the Russian arrived, I was a prospect looking to get patched in soon. What

McIntire and the Russian had done? They were the only two Alphas I'd ever seen able to pull it off. If they ever clashed, it would be like a nuclear blast, and the fallout would stick around for years.

McIntire's second had been introduced as Boomer. The guy wore this shit-eating grin like he knew something the rest of us really wanted to know. He didn't seem too worried that there were seven Wolves in the room, plus about ten human members. I figured if things went to shit, McIntire and the Russian would go one-on-one, and that left Boomer to face the rest of us. The dude didn't even break a sweat. Watching him closely I caught the feral glint in his eyes. Boomer had killed. More than once. And we didn't fucking scare him at all. Digger, Hardy, and I were all strong alphas. If this guy had been anywhere but standing next to McIntire and Russki, he would have been Alpha.

Shit. If we got out of this room without bloodshed, I'd call it a good night.

"You are here why?" The Russian didn't waste time on niceties.

"A couple of reasons. I heard the old man was dead. I wanted to confirm it."

The Russian smiled—the smile that meant death wasn't far behind—but didn't respond.

"I recognized the pelt. Neat trick."

Laughing, the Russian spread his hands in

a gesture that translated as, "What can I say?"

"What happened to my mother?"

Something flickered in the Russian's eyes, some emotion I couldn't translate. "They were mated. I was not." McIntire didn't move. "You know the Nightriders' tradition. I refused her." He glanced over to Hardy, who took up the story.

"I'm sorry, Sergeant Major. We kept an eye on her, making sure she had food, money. Then one day she just..." Hardy shrugged, and real sadness infiltrated his expression. "She'd gone into Kansas City. Stepped off the curb in front of a bus according to the cops. She was DOA."

Hardy seemed to know McIntire, since he called him by a military rank. Then I remembered he'd been a soldier too. Some sort of special unit. He ended up doing time in Iraq and Afghanistan before finally coming back to the Nightriders.

"I haven't been a sergeant major in years, Hardy. I'm just Mac now." Mac's voice dropped, but I could still hear it with my wolfy senses. "We need to talk. Just the Wolves."

Hardy's gaze slid over to the Russian when he spoke, "This *need* to talk, it is the only reason you are here?"

There was a soft *boom* and the floor

shuddered. Seconds later, the doors were kicked in, and a blonde woman armed to the teeth stood there wreathed in smoke.

Before anybody could react, Mac yelled, "Hannah, what the fuck?"

TWENTY

EASY

NOT ONE NIGHTRIDER MOVED. The woman was loaded for bear, and I recognized the look on her face. She'd kill the first one of us that so much as twitched—and do it without blinking. She gestured with a mean-ass automatic combat rifle, a weapon that could cut any one of us in half, and then she flashed a crazy smile at McIntire.

"I gawddamn told you, Mac. You had twenty fucking minutes. I'm double-parked." She moved her arm so the combat watch on her left wrist caught the light. "Time's up."

Not sure what to do, I watched the drama unfold like it was some action-adventure movie, and I was sitting in the front row eating popcorn. Then I realized Boomer was doubled over laughing.

"Shut up, Boomer," McIntire ordered.

"Hey, she's your mate, Mac."

The Russian relaxed, and one corner of his mouth tugged up in amusement. Huh. Something new and different—humor instead of deadly retaliation.

"Everything is fine, Hannah, except you owe these nice gentlemen some new doors."

The woman didn't look very contrite. In fact, her eyes did this shifty side-to-side thing. "Yeah, about that...and the two guys at the gate? Fuck it. They're gonna have headaches when they wake up."

That got us moving. Two of the human brothers edged toward the door, but halted when she pointed her weapon at them.

"You will let them pass." The Russian wasn't smiling now.

"Ah, Major Jackson?" Hardy took a half step toward her. "Things are a little tense right now, and we need guards on the gate. There are kids at risk."

Her entire attitude changed. She stepped closer to me and left a clear path through the door. "First Sergeant Tyree. Didn't expect to see you here. And it's just Hannah McIntire now."

"Yes, ma'am."

Every man in the room stared at Hardy. He'd earned his road name because he was a first degree hard ass, but he was acting all polite and shit with this woman. She turned to stare at me. "I may be old enough to be your mother, but I guaran-damn-tee I can shoot your balls off if you so much as breathe wrong."

I cut my eyes to Hardy. He nodded. Fuck.

Who was this bitch? Annie Oakley?

The Russian's laughter defused the situation. "I had planned to offer you the use of one of our women once our business is concluded. It is probably good you brought your own." He glanced at Boomer. "And you? I'm sure the whores are lining up to spread their legs for you."

"Thanks, but no thanks. Mated. And I'm pretty damn sure Annie gave Hannah permission to shoot my ass if I step out of line."

Tension ratcheted down while Mac and his mate glowered at each other. She finally shrugged. "Fine. It's your funeral." She glared at Boomer. "Annie is rather attached to that smart ass of yours. Make sure it stays in one piece because I won't be responsible if something happens to it."

"Uh..." I started to raise my hand like she was a fucking teacher, and I swear my balls shriveled a little when she looked at me. My respect for McIntire went up exponentially. "The old ladies are in the kitchen. You'd probably rather hang out with them than the club whores."

Da-yam. The look she gave me cut clear to the bone. There was no "if looks could kill" with her. Her glare was gawddamned deadly. And I sort of worried that I was steering her in the direction of Sam, Sunny, and Ginger.

The Russian released the regular members, ordering the cadre to stay. Mac's woman waited until the others filed out to hit the bar and the whores. She stared at her mate again, rolled her eyes, and left, closing the doors the best she was able behind her.

Then it dawned on me. Holy hell! They were true mates. The til-death-do-we-part-for-life mates. They could communicate psychically. I'd heard of the phenomenon, but it was the stuff of Bigfoot and Area 51 urban legends. I rubbed at my chest and realized my heart hurt a little because Sam and I didn't have that. Not really. I'd imagined that one time when she was fighting the Hell Dogs. It'd been a weird-ass feeling. What would it be like being so close to someone they lived in your head?

The Russian gestured for all of us to gather around the table at the end of the room where the council usually met. None of us sat down.

"What is this news you wish to share?"

"Have you ever heard of a corporation called Black Root?"

"Why would we be noticing corporate things? We are Nightriders."

"You are also Wolves and you aren't stupid, Sergei Rusakovavich."

Holy fuck. This guy knew the Russian's real name? I figured the dude was dead, but Russki just folded his arms across his chest.

"You are a man of many talents, Ian McIntire, but you are in my house now, and standing here only by my leave."

"Dammit, Sergei, this is important. Black Root has declared war on Wolves. On *all* Wolves. And they are after our pups."

Hardy shifted slightly and cleared his throat. At the Russian's nod, he spoke. "I thought your team handled that problem in Virginia, Mac."

"We cut off some of the heads, but the damn corporation is like a hydra. And there's government backing." Mac stared at Russki for a long moment. "You say you have a security situation involving kids. Are they pups?"

"No. Children of a woman who helped one of my men. A Hell Dog claims the little girl. She is under my personal protection, as is her half brother." The Russian shifted his gaze to me, and I read his message loud and clear. I kept my mouth shut about Sam.

Boomer cocked his head. "Hell Dogs? Have they raised their ugly heads again?" At nods all around, he glanced at Mac. "Remember those assholes in Texas? The Wolf Pack? They owed their allegiance to the Hell Dogs."

"Connections," Mac agreed.

The Russian, along with every one of us, studied both of the other men. "Explain."

"Several years ago, a small group of Wolf

Pack members were working with Black Root to kidnap Wolves and their pups. Including little girls who carried the Wolf gene. We thought we'd taken care of the situation after they kidnapped my son until we discovered another secret lab in the Louisiana bayous. They took a newly-mated couple, and when we rescued them, we discovered a child. She'd been held so long, she didn't remember her name."

Growls rumbled in the room, and a few of us had a little trouble maintaining our human forms. The Russian's eyes turned to ice. "Where is this child now?"

"One of my men and his mate adopted her. She's loved and safe now."

Digger had never looked deadlier when he asked, "What do they want with us?"

"What humans have always wanted." Mac's voice was filled with bitterness. "More strength. Better senses. Super soldiers. We stopped in for the reasons I've explained, Rusakovavich. I needed to confirm the old bastard who sired me was truly dead and to find out what happened to my mother. We plan to check in with various packs to give them the heads up. Black Root may not be called by that name any longer, but there are those out there who have taken up the banner. I know I don't have to say this to you, but I'm going to. Protect your people."

SAM

WHEN WE HEARD ONE of the whores scream, followed by what sounded like a small explosion, the three of us scrambled for the clubroom. The doors to the church room hung open and smoke swirled. I heard angry voices, but nobody came out. I exchanged looks with Sunny and Ginger. Were we under attack?

A few minutes later, four guys raced out and dashed through the front door, probably headed to the gate. Something was definitely going on, though when most of the other Nightriders walked out and bellied up to the bar, the three of us were pretty clueless. Then a woman walked out. Older, with blonde hair a bit longer than mine. She was dressed in jeans, a leather jacket, and carried a damn big gun. She rolled her eyes at the crap going on with the Nightriders and the whores and walked straight to us.

"You must be the old ladies."

Sunny, as the senior of us, nodded and cleared her throat. "Yeah. And?"

"I'm Hannah McIntire." She glanced over her shoulder and saw the wolf pelt on the wall. "Huh. So that's my dead father-in-law. Good riddance." She returned her attention to us, and I wanted to straighten up, like come to attention or something. "I need a beer."

That broke the ice a little, and we ushered her into the kitchen. Ginger snagged another round of beers, and we sat at the table. I noticed Hannah picked a seat allowing her see both the back exit, the door to the clubroom, and the windows.

Once again, Sunny was the one who spoke. "You...you're mated to that Alpha?"

"Mac? Yeah."

For a minute there, I thought Sunny was going to kneel beside the woman's chair and pay homage. Hannah twisted the top off her beer and took a deep swallow. "So..." She glanced at Sunny. "You belong to Repo. Any kids?"

A look of such sadness washed over Sunny's face my heart almost broke.

"No," she whispered.

Hannah made a move that surprised us all. She reached over and snagged Sunny in a hard hug. "I lost three, but I have a son, strong and in his teens."

Stunned, I curled into my seat and glanced over at Ginger. She had tears in her eyes when she said, "Radar and I...we haven't tried. I'm too scared."

Hannah watched me over the top of Sunny's head. "You're newly mated."

"Yeah. So?"

Her mouth thinned. "Turn around."

I did, and she growled as she read the

patch.

"Easy? The little pissant on the door? Hell, I should have shot his fucking balls off when I had the chance. He hasn't explained the facts of life, has he?"

"Excuse me?" I gave her my best go-to-hell face because nobody but me was going to touch Easy's balls, much less shoot them off.

The woman shook her head. "You need to talk to your mate. Fuckin' assholes. They forget all the important shit while their pheromones are swirling and their cocks are doing all the talking."

I laughed. I had to. "Gee, tell us what you really think."

"Go ahead and laugh, but I'll tell you something right now. We'll see if those assholes still in the meeting happen to mention what they're talking about in there to you all, who happen to be the ones most affected. Are there any other mates in this pack?"

"MC," Sunny corrected. "The Nightriders are an MC, not a pack. Not really. The inner cadre are Wolves, always have been. But there are human members too, and some of them have old ladies. We're the only three mated to Wolves. At least here. There are others in the club, nationwide."

"Here's the deal. There's a group out there looking to take Wolf DNA, and they're not too fucking particular how they get it. They've done bad shit. Kidnapping. Murder. And that includes kids. They took my son. We got him back and blew the facility to hell and back. They took a mated couple in our pack. We got them back. Along with a little girl they'd kept for years. Her father was a Wolf." She stared at each one of us, her gaze lingering until we acknowledged her words. "They took a group of soldiers and ran experiments on them. Only one survived. He wasn't born a Wolf, but he carried a recessive gene. They did bad shit to him and then they forced him to change. Your mates may not take the threat personally. You'd better."

I continued to stare at her. The woman believed every word she'd just said. "What are you saying?"

"That everyone mated to, descended from, or born a Wolf is in danger."

TWENTY-ONE

EASY

THE BLOOD MOON WANED without a challenge and only minor bloodshed, mostly due to heavy doses of booze and testosterone. The cadre exhaled a collective breath of relief. Since we'd delivered Lumpy, and left him nailed to the Hell Dogs' front gate, they'd been noticeably absent. Rumors filtered in about a rogue MC cruising through the region—one full of guys so tough not even the Nightriders would go up against them—and that was the reason the Dogs were laying low.

Nightrider chapters snuffed that shit right out. Rogue MC, yeah. Dogs pissing themselves and hiding, damn straight. But we made sure everyone knew the rogues were passing through with the Russian's permission and that they'd come to him first to get that consent.

A month passed, and life settled back into a normal rhythm. Well, normal for us. I finally got off the shit list, but Repo was still on it, despite Sunny making nice with Sam. He was currently hiding out from the cops.

Sandhog ran the Nightriders' payday loan company. Like his name, Repo collected collateral when the jerkwads missed a payment. He'd gone after a guy's Jaguar, and the guy got run over. Wasn't Repo's fault the idiot jumped in front of the wrecker. Cops thought different.

Sam felt sorry for Sunny so she and the kids spent a lot of time with her. Maybe they'd make up and be nice. Men? We just beat the crap out of each other. Women had to do this whole emotional dance thing that made no fucking sense to me or any other male I knew.

I mostly worked for Ryder Bail Bonds. Radar managed the place, and he was currently kicked back at his desk drinking a beer. I'd settled into another chair and had my boots propped on the corner of said desk when my phone buzzed. Sam.

"Hey, baby."

"Are you working tonight?"

"Love you too."

That made her laugh. "Get your mind out of the bedroom, you freak. That's not why I'm asking. I mean, jeez. Didn't you get enough this morning before you left the house?"

"Darlin', I can never get enough of your sweet pussy."

"You better be alone, pervert."

I winked at Radar, and he saluted me with

his bottle. "You love it when I talk dirty to you. Want me to tell you how I'm going to fuck you tonight when I get home?"

"Easy!"

"Nothin' easy about it, babe. I'm gonna bend you over the couch and fuck you until your cum drips down your legs. Then I'm gonna use your cum to lube up that sweet ass of yours and finger fuck it while I—"

"EASY! Shut. Up. Someone's there. I know it."

I laughed. Couldn't help it. I could feel her blushin' through the phone.

"Shut up. Just shut up. And don't you dare tell me who's sitting there listening because I will never be able to face them again. You are so not getting any tonight."

I made kissing noises, and she finally laughed. "Sadly, sweet Sam, I do have to work tonight. Fucker didn't show up to court today. He works the night shift at some plant up in North Kansas City. It's payday so he'll be there to pick up his check. I should be home by midnight. The kids will be asleep, and I can make some sweet, sweet lovin' to my woman."

"Oh."

Shit. "Oh" ranked right up there with "fine" in the lexicon of things women say when they aren't happy. "Sam?"

"Never mind."

Crap. From bad to worse. "Ah, darlin'? You need to talk to me. What's up?"

A huge sigh. Why do women do that? Being a Wolf, I could be patient. I waited.

"It's just that Sunny's all alone and stuff, and I thought maybe if you weren't working, you could watch the kids, and Sunny and I could go catch a movie. There's a new flick we both want to see and..." Another big sigh.

Radar rolled his eyes and mouthed the name of the latest chick flick. "Why don't you get a babysitter?" I glanced at Radar, but he was sitting up shaking his head and making pumping motions with his hand. Yeah, he had plans to nail Ginger tonight. "How 'bout Teri?"

"I'll give her a call. I should beat you home so don't go getting that handsome face of yours messed up. I might just have plans for it later." She made kissy noises back at me and ended the call.

By midnight, my ass was numb from sitting in the Hummer. My runner hadn't shown up. The dickwad lived from paycheck to paycheck so he couldn't run far without this cash. I was about to call it quits when an old junker pulled up. A frowzy redhead climbed out and headed inside. A quick scan of the file confirmed her identity. She'd lead me straight to her boyfriend, I'd put him in cuffs, drop him off at county jail, and head home to Sam.

My phone buzzed, and I answered without looking, figuring it was Sam. "You better be naked in bed, baby, I'll be home in an hour."

"Uhm...Easy?"

Fuck. "Teri?"

"I take it Sam isn't with you."

"Not hardly. Isn't she home?"

"No. Not yet. She was supposed to be home by eleven at the latest. I have an early class tomorrow. She and Sunny promised they wouldn't be late."

"Did you call her?" The back of my neck itched, and my gut tightened.

"Well, d'uh. I called them both. Neither answered. I thought maybe the movie ran late, but I called the megaplex. Their movie ended on time, and there wasn't another showing in that theater. I'm getting worried, Easy. I called Sandy, and he's coming over to stay with me and the kids."

My phone indicated another incoming call. Maybe it was Sam. "I'll call you back, Teri." I ended and answered with two swipes of my finger. "Sam?"

"Easy, you come to compound. Now."

The Russian, his accent thick. That only happened when shit hit the fan.

🐾 🐾 🐾 🐾

I WATCHED THE VIDEO the Hell Dogs had sent, my face a frozen mask. Thank fuck Repo wasn't here. One look at Sunny's face and he would have gone howling off half-cocked. My wolf howled too, but I'd gone stone cold like Russki. I would kill a Hell Dog for every mark they put on Sam. I would castrate every man who touched her, feeding them their own balls as I hammered railroad spikes through their dicks.

They took my mate. There wasn't enough pain in the world to inflict on them that would ever come close to what they deserved.

We don't talk about what we are, especially to outsiders. The bitches who hang around the clubhouse want to take a walk on the wild side, but they don't know how wild we can get. We're predators. We hunt. We bleed our prey and drink the sweet, hot blood. It's who and what we are. Some of us are more...domesticated than others, but even those Wolves will gut an enemy without a thought. Don't fuck with what's ours. Too bad the Hell Dogs didn't get the memo. They came into our territory. And they took what was mine. I'd kill every last motherfucking one of them to get Sam back.

The Russian knew what was going on in my head. He'd already ordered the whores out of the building. He sent the human brothers to the armory and put out the call for reinforcements. In the time it took Radar to track our women, the Nightrider nation would be mobilized for war. Scorched earth. There wouldn't be a Hell Dog left breathing after we finished with them.

SAM

THE HELL DOGS SNATCHED us in the parking lot of the movie complex. Sunny and I never had a chance. Tied up, gagged, and blindfolded, I had no idea where they took us. It wasn't a long trip nor did they make many turns. I didn't care. As soon as we got free, I'd get us home. Somehow.

They dragged us into what I discovered was a warehouse once they took off the blindfold. Two Hell Dogs held me by the arms, my hands bound in front of me. A third Dog slipped a collar and leash on Sunny. Another biker strolled in, one who reminded me of the Russian only colder. The Dogs called him Angel and all but turned belly up in submission. Approaching Sunny, he leaned close, and sniffed her. He whispered something I couldn't hear and a look of stark terror crossed her face. He took the leash, jerked hard enough Sunny almost fell, then led her away.

"No!" I screamed it over and over. "Leave her alone, you son of a bitch! Don't touch her!" No matter how much I fought—screaming, biting, and kicking—I couldn't get free to help her. They disappeared through a door into what looked like an office.

My captors knocked me off my feet and kicked me a couple of times. Somebody grabbed me by the hair and yanked me across the floor. I must have blacked out for awhile because the next thing I knew, I was all but swinging by a hook. The ropes around my wrists had been looped over it, and I could just keep my toes on the concrete floor.

I wore an old pair of fatigues, and my phone was still in one of the side cargo pockets. I'd turned the ringer off when the movie started, but I hadn't powered off the phone. That phone was my salvation. There was a reason Radar got his name. He was the best skip tracer in the business, and he had the computer savvy to locate and track my cell signal. As soon as Sunny and I didn't show at home, they'd start looking. All I had to do was hold on. Easy would come. He had to.

I shut down at some point. My brain couldn't handle what those bastards did to me. I remembered watching them beat Sunny. Sweet, dear Sunny who wasn't always nice, but who was trying to be my friend again. The Hell Dogs punched her in the face, blackening both her eyes, breaking her nose, and splitting her lip. Oddly, they never once landed a body blow. Oh, they felt her up, twisting her breasts until she cried out. They chained her in the corner of this horrible room that smelled of piss and shit and vomit. Ripping off her shirt and bra, they didn't rape her. For that I was grateful. They would break me open, but Sunny? Sunny would die if they touched her like that. She was Repo's mate. For life. What she'd told me was a *true* mate—something deeper and far more mystical than just mating with a Wolf.

I remembered searing heat and pain beyond any I'd ever experience. I remembered screaming until no sound came from my throat. Then all I could remember was blessed darkness.

When I opened my eyes, the Bastard was there. I'd been tied to a table, naked. Leering at me, he squeezed my breasts and jammed his fingers inside me. He had his dick out in his hands, ready to ram into me, but that uber-scary biker walked in and stopped him by shoving the Bastard away. Angel bent over and sniffed me, and his eyes lit up with possessive sparks.

"No man will fuck her, not with his dick."

"Fuck you," the Bastard argued. "I've been waiting months to fuck this bitch." He shut up fast when the guy growled, fisted one hand in the Bastard's cut and lifted him off the floor.

"I'll fuck *you* if your dick touches this cunt. Stick whatever the hell gets you off up her cunt so long as it isn't a human cock. Choke her with your cum, but I will butt fuck any man who's dick gets between her legs. Do you understand?"

The Bastard whimpered something that sounded like, "Yes, sir," right before the guy tossed him like a bag of garbage against the wall. Angel stood between my legs and stared at me. He was so big, he blocked everything else in the room. "You are mated, but I don't give a flying shit. You're close to being fertile and when you are, I'm going to fuck your cunt until you're pregnant."

Something dark and predatory flickered in his eyes, and I knew. He wasn't human. He was a Wolf. He smiled, and I felt like I'd been flash frozen. I was still shivering when the torture started again. I didn't scream. Sunny was still curled up in the corner, and I refused to make it worse for her. Not that I was any big hero or anything. I just figured she might still be alive when the Nightriders came for us. They'd come. I never had any doubt. I also refused to give these bastards any satisfaction by screaming, even if my screams were silent because I had no voice left.

I passed out again, tasting blood from biting the insides of my cheeks, my tongue, my lips. I was beyond pain, beyond anything. White noise filled my brain. I drifted along, occasionally aware of men doing things to me, but the white noise always came back, always took me far away where I couldn't feel.

Time had no meaning, but the white noise lessened and another sound intruded. Loud. Rumbling. Like rolling thunder. Motorcycles. Hundreds of them. At least to my ears. Had Easy come? He'd promised. There under the stars, he promised he would always find me, even if he had to ride through the fires of hell to get to me. He said he'd never leave me, that I was his and he was mine. I'd believed him. My sanity danced on a tightrope, an umbrella in one hand, and no net down below. If I fell, there would be no coming back from the madness.

The noise filled my head, but echoing it came music, and with the notes, words. I knew this song. The Moody Blues sang it. *Nights in White Satin.* The words became clearer, and I sang them—or thought I did— finding their truth. And I realized my own truth. If I broke because I fell off the tightrope, knowing my parasol would not float me to earth so that I would break upon the jagged rocks of this reality, I knew that Easy would die. Mates. For life.

No. He would not die. Could not die. I refused to let him. He was mine. And I loved him. I whispered the words to him in my mind, hoping they found their way through the white satin cocooning me. Even as I dreamed of motorcycles roaring through flames, I whispered the words.

Always, Easy, I will love you. My life. My heart.

TWENTY-TWO

RUSSKI

WE SWEPT OVER THE HILL, a tide of avenging Cossacks on iron horses. Two hundred Nightriders had come immediately to rescue the mates of their brothers. Thousands more answered my declaration of war against the Hell Dogs. Highways would turn to rivers of blood as we hunted down our enemies.

As soon he received word of his mate's predicament, Repo came out of hiding. He would face prison with a grim face if the police discovered him, but he would not stay behind when his mate and his pup were threatened. He and Sunny had told no one of her pregnancy before now. The Nightriders were prepared to mourn a life cut short in the womb, and then avenge the innocent with fire and blood.

Easy wore the death's head mask with the ease of a man born to its burdens. His mate had changed him, sharpening some edges, softening others. He was no longer carefree. These past months haunted his soul, and I knew I would have to put him down if we found his mate dead. Easy would turn rogue and, as much as I understood the emotions feeding his rage, it was bad business.

Of the fifty Hell Dogs left behind to guard the warehouse, all but a handful died swiftly. Four were tortured to find where the coward known as Fallen Angel had rabbited. The fifth was mine. The Bastard, the nightmare stalking a little girl's dreams.

EASY

BLOOD. SO DAMN MUCH BLOOD. I wanted to kill the fucking Hell Dog again. I wanted to shift and let my wolf savage the sumbitch. Right after I threw up. We fought our way to the room where they were holding the girls. Repo spotted Sunny crouched in the corner, an iron shackle around her neck.

I just stood there staring at Sam. She was lashed to a table, her hips at the edge, her ankles tied to the legs. There wasn't an inch of her that wasn't black, blue or bloody. My wolf howled, rage bleeding over into anguish. I wanted to rip out the heart of every gawddamned Hell Dog and feast on their guts.

My knife was in my hand. I didn't remember drawing it from its sheath. I cut Sam free, but I was scared to touch her. I didn't want to hurt her any more than she already was. "Ah, baby, I'm so fucking sorry." They'd tortured her because of me. Because of the Nightriders.

She got one eye open and focused on me. Her voice was a raspy whisper. "Easy?"

Her poor lips, so swollen and cut. How could she even talk?

"It's me, baby. You're safe now. I'm gonna take care of you."

A sound ripped from her throat. I didn't know if it was a moan, a cry...or maybe it was a laugh. "Here you are, larger than life. My hero."

My heart shredded. I was no hero. I'd failed her. "C'mon, sweetheart. We'll get out of here. Hardy will fix you." I hoped to hell the Nightrider medic could. She was so fucking broken. "If he can't, Doc Carson will."

I picked her up, cradled her, her wince of pain arrowing through my heart.

"S'okay, Easy. You came."

"Always, Sam. I'll always come for you. You're mine."

"Yes, yours. Always."

My life. My love.

Her voice echoed in my head. Not the broken, rusty sound rasping out of her throat. *Her* voice. The one that touched me when I slept, the one that turned me hard when her words stroked me as I woke.

I will always find you. No matter where you

are. I love you, Sam. With everything I am.

She smiled, as much as her tattered lips could. She'd heard me. My heart and soul shredded...exploded, and then they merged, becoming something new. Something special. The truth of a true mating was so much...more than I'd ever imagined.

Repo carried Sunny out. The Hummer had been pulled inside the warehouse. Repo gently placed her in the backseat while Hardy asked questions—the same questions he'd be asking Sam. The same questions that would shred my self-control. I was hanging on by sheer stubbornness.

When I tried to put her on the seat next to Sunny, Sam refused to let go. She whimpered when Hardy touched her and buried her face against my chest. Deadhead, the Topeka chapter president, appeared. Keeping his eyes averted, he passed over two silver solar blankets.

"Marie always makes me pack an emergency kit in the saddlebags," he explained.

Hardy took the blankets and squeezed Deadhead's shoulder. "The girls appreciate it. And Marie's foresight. Thanks, man."

After Repo and I got our mates covered, Deadhead looked up. Expression fierce, eyes burning, he made a promise. "These motherfuckers are dead. I'll personally hand you the balls, dicks, and heads of every damned Hell Dog Topeka hunts down. A man doesn't do this shit to a woman." Deadhead turned on his heel and stomped away.

Hardy repacked his emergency first aid kit and stowed it in the back. "I've already called Doc Carson. He'll meet us at the clinic."

Twenty brothers escorted us to Doc's place, forming a phalanx of motorcycles that kept the public at bay. The scanner we ran in the Hummer already told us what we needed to know. Local LEOs were running scared. A Nightrider war was something they wanted nothing to do with. Orders went out from the governor's office to every law enforcement officer in the state—as long as civilians were left alone, the cops were not to engage. That was good. They'd all live to go home to their families.

RUSSKI

WITH INFINITE CARE, I crushed the Bastard's nuts in my hand. He occupied the table where Easy had found Sam. Gravedigger first insisted on washing it down with bleach before we tied the man in Samantha's place.

"I don't want her blood fouled by this fucker's stench."

That Digger then poured bleach into the Bastard's open wounds was just a bonus. I would extract the information we needed and reward the Bastard with exquisite pain delivered by my hand. Submissives lined up to beg for my not-so-tender care at Nightshades. My skills were crafted by a master in the art of pain. He prepared me to embrace it in order to learn to bestow pain in the perfect way. He taught me to read my subjects. To understand every nuance of their souls. I transported them to the ultimate edge before rescuing them from themselves, anchoring their psyches on the threshold of excruciating insanity. I was four when his lessons began.

My mentor named me his crowning achievement—a Dom existing only to bring punishment and pain to those who required such for release. A Dom who achieved no sexual gratification—no emotional fulfillment—from the acts inflicted. And by doing so, he created in me the perfect instrument. Enforcer. Assassin. Torturer. Simply a tool for my Russkaya Mafiya masters to exploit. Until I escaped.

I returned my attentions to the Bastard. "You will tell me why the child of Sarah Prescott is of such importance to you."

"Fuck you."

I altered my touch slightly. The man at my mercy screamed. "Again." Another squeeze. I continued until he wept, his ankles and wrists bloody from his struggles against the barbed wire Digger had used to bind him.

"Why does the one you call Fallen Angel wish to own this child?"

A knife appeared in Digger's hand. He flashed it before the Bastard's eyes. "I think he wants a little edge play."

I accepted the stiletto, spread the Bastard's butt cheeks, and flicked my wrist, the tip of the knife nicking the perineum ridge between scrotum and rectum. "*Da?* This is something you enjoy, my friend? No? Then perhaps you will share the answers to my questions." I teased the knife across his groin, leaving a red trail. The next line of blood touched the base of his dick.

"Stop! Oh, fucking please stop. The little bitch is mine. I'm her goddamn father."

"Why is this important?" I pressed the tip of the stiletto into the head of his dick with just enough pressure to draw a tiny bead of blood.

The bastard screamed again, but did not thrash. When he could speak, he confirmed my own suspicions.

"My old man. He raped my whore of a mother. He was supposed to be some hot shit, but his fancy DNA skipped me. As soon as he figured that out, he disappeared."

My mask remained in place, but the waves of anger flowing from Digger washed against my control. I removed the knife. The Bastard was already dead yet was too stupid to understand. He believed he would survive my attentions. I had one last promise to keep. To discover the identity and location of the Hell Dogs' president—the one called Fallen Angel.

TWENTY-THREE

EASY

THE RUSSIAN LIFTED my mutilated hands, examining them closely before glancing at the rough concrete wall covered in blood. Hardy peered over his shoulder.

"Christ, Easy. What the fuck did you do?" Grabbing his medic's kit, Hardy pulled out a bottle of disinfectant.

I didn't flinch when he poured that crap over the mangled skin stretched across my swollen knuckles. My eyes stayed glued to Russki's face.

His gaze held mine when he spoke. "I cannot turn back time, Easy. To undo what's been done is impossible."

"Yeah, no shit." I didn't care if I was showing disrespect to the Nightriders' president, to my Alpha. The Russian would just have to get over it. Rage—raw and primal—churned inside me looking for an outlet. He knew that, knew why I had destroyed my hands. I was a Wolf. I would heal, good as new. But not Sam. Sam was human, and those fuckers had broken her. A month had passed since the rescue, and still the fires raged inside me.

I'd sat there, that night, beside the hospital bed where the woman who was my everything lay broken and bleeding. I listened as she told Doc Carson what the Bastard had done to her—the parts she could remember. Her physical injuries were healing. Her fertile period had come and gone. My wolf wanted to claim her, to make babies with her. But I was more than the wolf. I was a man, and I saw her flinch when I touched her. I saw the pain she carried every fucking day. I heard her crying into her pillow every night and fucking knew I'd make it worse if I touched her, held her.

She finally admitted what Angel had said to her. That's why I left town during her fertility. Russki told her it was club business, and she didn't ask. I just couldn't stand to be in the same fucking room with her and not be able to love her, to know that she would never have children with me because I couldn't fucking touch her and ease her pain.

Russki gripped my shoulder, jerking me back into the bullshit of my reality.

"We will exact our revenge, Easy. The Hell Dogs who took Samantha and Sunny will die. All of them."

"Damn straight they will." We'd killed the Dogs left behind when we rescued the girls.

We'd caught the Bastard. When the Russian finished torturing him for answers, Gravedigger strung the asshole's guts like party streamers in that room where Sam had been tortured. Most of the Dogs ran like the cowards they were. Our chapters still hunted them down, one by one, getting closer to the inner circle with each kill. Angel. His second. Others. I would hunt each one and rip out their throats. I had the scent of every man who'd touched Sam burning in my nose.

I'd gone back that night, after Sam was sedated and asleep. I saw Gravedigger's handiwork and wished I'd been the one to eviscerate the scumfuck. The Bastard had threatened my little girl, my son. He'd killed their mother and hurt my mate. Noni and Jonah were mine now—or would be as soon as Sam was fully healed, and we could appear in court for the finalization of their adoption.

The Russian watched me, and I straightened my spine and shoulders, coming to attention. Yeah, I'd lost it and beat the crap out of that wall, but I was back in control. And until Sam healed, I'd stick close. The Hell Dogs would never get another chance to hurt her.

I forced air into my lungs, forced my fists— formed by instinct—to spread wide and then relax to work out the soreness radiating all the way up to my shoulders. Sam wasn't the only one who'd been hurt. Repo's old lady had been in that room too, had been badly beaten. I hadn't asked before now and guilt burned in my gut. "How's Sunny?"

"Are you ready to hear this?"

The Russian stood deceptively loose. The man was fucking fast, and he'd take me down in heartbeat if I lost my shit. He didn't need Hardy standing there or Gravedigger, who'd moved into the shadows to watch and listen. I nodded, one short, quick dip of my chin, not trusting any words that might escape.

"They beat her, touched her, but did not rape her."

I swallowed. Hard. Repo would have gone ape-shit crazy if they had. She was his mate, like Sam was mine.

"Angel knew she was carrying Repo's child. A son."

His words didn't sink in at first. I stared at him until comprehension hit. "Son? A Wolf?"

Russki's expression confirmed it. "Angel told Sunny he would keep her as a pet, then would rip the child from her womb and raise it as his own."

"Aw shit." My gut clenched. "He mindfucked both of them."

"They leave for the Gulf in the morning, Repo and Sunny."

"Good." Corpus Christi was Repo's home chapter. The brothers down there would look after and protect them.

Hardy cleared his throat. I cut him off before he could say the words. "I already know." Hollywood broke the news to me right before I hit the wall. The fucking Hell Dogs had burned down our house. The kitchen Sam loved. All the toys and clothes I made Jonah and Noni leave behind when I moved them back into the Barracks for safety. I didn't know how to tell her. Tell them. Every home they'd ever had got ripped away. Destroyed. And I'd had a hand in almost all of it.

"You think too hard for a Wolf, Easy."

I couldn't meet Russki's gaze. "Hard not to, boss. I'm to blame for most of this."

The fucker laughed. When I looked up and glared, he laughed even harder and clapped Hardy on the shoulder.

"This is fine joke our Easy makes, *da*? He is such a Wolf that the world spins around him. What do you think of his arrogance, Hardy?"

Hardy was smart enough to keep his mouth shut.

"What? Because you were shot and taken in by Sarah Prescott, you somehow set everything in motion? This is the conceit of a fool."

"Maybe."

"Say you died. There beside the road. What would happen to Noni, to Jonah when the

Bastard found them? It was not you that led the Hell Dogs to that place. They were looking already. They want the girl. She is worth a great deal of money. Because you were there, they did not get her. They will not get her now. Do you think of this, Elijah? Maybe this is the way it was to be. Me? I don't believe in Fate. But look at you. You have a mate. Two children."

I wanted to say something, but when I opened my mouth, nothing came out except, "Well. Fuck."

That just made Russki and Hardy both laugh. "Our Easy is a man of many words, Hardy."

The two of them left me to stew, with Hardy calling back over his shoulder, "Put some ice on those hands."

Fucking d'uh. I cleaned up, wandered into the clubroom. The atmosphere was tense. Too much testosterone confined in close quarters did that. The club whores had been banned for the duration. I snagged a bottle of Irish and a bar towel full of ice from the machine and headed back to the garage. The kids' play fort distracted me. I climbed up inside, beneath the striped awning. Bracing my back against one wall, I could peer out over the top and watch other Nightriders come and go. I was invisible. I'd never really been a kid and damn sure never had a place like this. It was kinda cool. Curling up with my liquid security blanket, I understood the appeal.

I finally went to Sam. Awakened by my arrival, she stared at me from behind swollen eyes, like an abused dog.

"What do you want from me?" she whispered through lips still showing the trauma she'd suffered.

"Nothing, baby. I just want to take care of you. To love you."

"Why?"

"Because I do, Sam. You're mine. No matter what."

"I can't, Easy. I can't do this."

"Shh, baby."

"Please don't make me come out there."

"You don't have to, baby. Can I crawl in there with you?" I could give her this, if nothing else.

Understanding lit her eyes. She nodded. We'd hide here until she was ready to face the world again. We'd survive, together.

Chapter 24

EASY

THE HANDS THAT had pounded the wall
with rage until they bled were gentle when
they touched her. I remained terrified I'd hurt
Sam even more. She had altered me in ways I
didn't understand. I'd been rough, crude
before she came into my life. Part of me
wanted to take her, own her, show the world
she was mine. Instead, I reined in those
needs, made sure my hands were tender. I
planned to just hold her, but she was the one
who drew me down, held me. She was the one
who sighed when I sighed. We would comfort
each other for now. I could do that. The need
for revenge burned like acid through my
blood, but I would hold on. I would remain
gentle for this remarkable woman. *My*
woman. My *mate*.

Her lips met mine, parted in the softest,
sweetest of joinings. Her hands stroked my
chest, along the hard ridges of muscle as I fit
my body to hers. I parted the nightgown she
wore, but I couldn't hide my wince at the

sight of her bruises. Fucking Hell Dogs. They'd marked her. Hurt her. Her injuries still visible weeks later.

Sam's hand fluttered against my cheek. "Shhh," she murmured.

I'd meant to comfort her, to prove how much she was loved, but my mate was showing me. I buried my nose in the hollow of her throat and inhaled deeply, filling my lungs with her scent. Vanilla from her shampoo. A hint of cedar from her soap. But underneath the fake stuff was the real her. She smelled of honeysuckle—sweet, but not cloying—and beneath the nectar the acrid tang of gunpowder. This scent was uniquely hers. It defined her. I would be able to find her anywhere in the world by her scent alone.

Trailing my lips down her flesh, I touched each bruise, trying to kiss away the marks, to make it all better. I wanted to heal her, take away her pain, and I was steeped in the scent and feel of her. I traced fingertips over her slight curves, hesitating when she sighed or trembled, watching pleasure bloom on her face.

"Sweet Sam." My lips found hers again, rubbed gently. "So beautiful."

"I'm not beautiful."

My lips curled against hers. "This isn't the time to argue." I closed my hand lightly over her breast, and I watched her eyes. "Perfect.

You fit my hand, just like this." I flicked a thumb over her nipple, and her breath hitched. "Those eyes of yours, like the ocean. Deep. Restless. How can they see everything but what I see when I look at you?"

I lowered my head to taste her mouth. "Soft. Irresistible. Stubborn." I skimmed my tongue over the hollow under her chin. "I love this spot," I whispered. "My Sam, so perfect." I ran my hand down the length of her. And when I cupped her pussy, she was already wet. "Let go, baby. Come for me."

She finally did, under my gentle attention as she became helpless beneath my hands, with a breathy moan that signaled the pleasure of her surrender.

I wanted to make her feel beautiful. Make her understand how important she was, that she was my other half, and together we were whole. She reached for me, rolling with me in a dance sensual and timeless. She touched and tasted and gave as I did. Lost herself in me.

When she rose to me, when I slid inside her, her eyes blurred with tears.

"Don't." I pressed my cheek to hers. "Ah, don't." Her tears would ruin me.

"Shh." She framed my face, let the tears come. "This is right. Perfect. Can't you see?" She lifted to me again, rolling her hips. "Can't you feel? I love the weight of you, the way your body fits mine. I love the taste of you, the way you smell." She smiled even as the tears sparkled on her cheeks. "You make me beautiful. Being with you makes me beautiful. You don't see my scars."

She held my face in her hands, and we moved together, took that hot, ragged climb to the peak. There was tenderness in her kisses, and I gave it back to her with slow, sliding caresses. When I felt her quiver, saw her eyes go to midnight, I hoped she understood.

"Yes." The word whispered at the edge of my hearing.

After, as we lay quietly wrapped in each other, I waited for her to go limp, to slide away from consciousness, so I knew she slept. When she did, I brushed a kiss over her hair. "I love you."

Even in the dark, I saw the curve of her lips. Yes, she understood.

Chapter 25

SAM

A DAY. Well, a day and two nights. Easy just held me, there in his bed. Our bed. With the covers over our heads like two five-year-olds afraid of the monsters in the closet. We made love again. Sweet and tender like before. He treated me like fine china, fearing he would chip me or break me into pieces. He could only do that if he left me.

I wanted what we had before. I wanted the wild sex, the kids' laughter, our house. I rubbed my nose against his side. Easy was ticklish there, and my action got a jerk and exhalation from him. Then I bit him. Not hard, just a quick nip. I wanted to get back to normal—well, normal for us.

Flipping on top of him, I straddled his morning wood and smiled. Most guys were semi-hard first thing. My Easy? Oh heck no. He was stiff and throbbing. I looked down, and a drop of pre-cum already dotted the head of his cock.

"Rise and shine, big boy."

Easy snored. I rubbed my thumb over his

penis, spreading cum so his skin slickened to wet silk. His eyes opened to slits.

"What do you think you're doing?"

"I don't think, I know. I'm going to fuck my mate."

His blue Husky eyes glittered, and I caught a glimpse of the wolf beneath his gaze. Good. I wanted him wild. He'd been pussy-footing around me long enough. I rose up on my knees, rubbing my own slick sex up the length of him. His cock jerked against me.

Easy's hands gripped my waist, but I planted one hand on his chest and used the other to line up his erection with my entrance. I sank down on him, watched his eyes go wide, listened to a satisfied growl rumble in his chest.

"Sam?"

"Shh. It's okay. I'm not going to break."

His expression looked so hopeful, my heart stuttered. How bad off had I been for the past few weeks? How much had Easy, our kids, and everyone else suffered because I'd withdrawn into my fears?

"I promise, Easy. Love me. Make love to me. Hard. Fast. Like we did before. I need you to be you. So I can be me."

With my words, the genteel veneer dropped away, and my man was back. Wolfish. Demanding. Claiming what was his—me.

In a flash, I was on my back, my ankles

hooked around his back. His thick cock filled me, heated me from the inside out, warming all the places I'd let grow cold while I hid from my panic.

This is what I needed to heal. My man surging into me, his eyes holding my gaze, his hunger a thing alive and demanding filling the voids within us both. I saw it all so clearly now. His hesitancy. His fear. He'd believed he'd failed me, broken his promise. But he hadn't. He'd come for me. Found me. Brought me home.

Running my hand across the rippling muscles of his back, I pulled him closer, fit his body to mine, two pieces of the same puzzle, whole only when we were joined in our hearts and our minds.

I love you.

His eyes widened, and one of those darn dimples that made him so sexy peeked from the corner of his smile.

"I know, babe."

"Ha! Cocky much?"

He stopped, hips still, buried deep inside. Then his cock throbbed. Once. My eyes glazed over. "Oh, yeah, babe. I damn sure am."

I pinched his butt. "Move."

"Yes, ma'am."

He rolled his hips, arched, pulled all but free of me, and then surged forward, deep, connecting us on levels I'd never known existed.

"Fuck, baby."

"Yes, please."

He laughed, a rather helpless sound, and then he couldn't stop. He drove into my depths time and time again. I arched my hips to meet his thrusts. I could no longer control my inner muscles, had lost all ability to finesse our love-making. This was something raw. Primal. This was the wolf taking his mate. And I gloried in it.

When my climax broke, followed a nanosecond later by his, I was left boneless. Mindless. Easy existed. His warmth wrapped me in a cocoon, his rough-haired skin rubbed against my hyper-sensitive skin, abrading, teasing.

"Everything," he wheezed. "Everything I am."

We dozed again, after he managed to slide off me and tug me close to spoon. His breath tickled the back of my neck, keeping me in a half-waking state. I thought I misheard when he murmured against my skin.

"Marry me, Sam."

"I thought we were…at least in the eyes of the club."

"You're mine for life, baby. But I want the rest of the world to know. I want it legal. I want the kids to be legal. No one can take you or them away from me."

"Okay."

His lashes fluttered against my skin. "Just *okay*?"

"Well, you didn't exactly ask. So okay. I'll marry you."

Easy laughed, and something eased in my chest. Yes. We would get back to normal. We'd been inching that direction, feeling our uncertain way, but with his deep chuckle, I knew we were us again.

EASY

I MADE A LIST in my head. Get marriage license. Get another set of the adoption papers for the kids. They'd gone up in smoke with the rest of our stuff. Tell Sam the house was gone. Tell Sam the Bastard was dead. Tell Sam that Sunny was pregnant and that she and Repo were gone.

"You're thinking too hard. Just tell me."

I rolled to my back and repositioned her body so she was snuggled against my side and I could see her face. "A lot has happened, Sam."

A sort of gigglesnort sound erupted from her. "Is this where I say d'uh?"

Trying to smile, I knew I didn't succeed when her expression sobered. I blurted, "The Russian and Gravedigger killed the Bastard. The night we rescued you."

"Good." No hesitation, but something

shifted in the depths of her blue gaze. Concern, followed by comprehension. "You wanted to do it."

"Yeah. I did. But I was with you. I couldn't leave you. They got the info they needed from him, and they made sure he paid for what he'd done. To your sister. The kids. You."

She nodded, her chin easing over my skin. "What else?"

"Sunny and Repo. They're gone."

Sam bit her lips and sucked in a breath. "Gone?" Her voice quivered.

"S'okay, babe. Bad choice of words. Turns out Sunny's pregnant. She and Repo have gone to Corpus Christi. The chapter down there will take care of them, keep them safe until the baby's born. Then they'll come back."

Her inhale eased the tension in her body. "Still waiting for that other shoe."

"Our house. The fucking Hell Dogs burned it down."

She stilled beside me, not even breathing. "We lost everything?"

"Everything that wasn't important. You're here. The kids are safe. That's all that matters. Everything else can be fixed. Already in the works, in fact."

"What do you mean?"

"Did you meet Marie? She's Deadhead's old lady."

"From Topeka."

"Yeah. She's organizing a party for the kids. She's calling it something ridiculous, a 'It's Not Your Birthday' party. To get clothes and books and toys for them." I felt Sam's smile against my skin. That was a good sign. "And the chapters, all of them, they're doing poker runs and shit to raise money to rebuild the house. A crew is already working to clear out everything. One of the Arkansas brothers is a builder. He's bringing his crew up. It'll take a couple of months, but we'll have our house back."

"Where will we live until then?" She pushed up and sat cross-legged. I damn sure liked the view of her pussy. She blushed, pulled a pillow into her lap, and rolled her eyes. "Focus, Easy. We can't stay here. I know you love these guys, but it's not really a good place for Jonah and Noni. Not twenty-four seven."

"Repo offered their house to us. Temporarily. Once you feel ready."

Sam contemplated the idea for a long minute. "The kids are familiar with it, so it won't be like moving somewhere strange."

I snuck my hand under the pillow and teased her thigh. She slapped at it, but her eyes twinkled. I was so fucking relieved. She was taking all this news a hellava lot better than I thought she would.

"What else?"

"The kids. Adopting them." I didn't want to go there, but I had to.

"I thought we'd already agreed on that."

Her brow did this little scrunched up thing, and I sat up so I could kiss the wrinkles away. Leaning back against the headboard, I decided to just lay it on the line. "Pretty Woman. Sarah. She's still in the morgue."

Her face crumpled, and I pulled her down against my chest where I could hold and pet her.

"I...I forgot. Oh, God, Easy. How could I forget about my own sister? My twin!"

I brushed her cheek with my fingertips and found tears. "Shh, baby. S'not like you've had much time to take a breath since she died. Besides, we needed things to settle down so the cops wouldn't investigate us. I knew we'd get justice for her. The Bastard is dead. The kids are safe. You're safe. We'll go together. After we're married. Then you can file the papers for custody, and we'll adopt Jonah and Noni. They'll be ours, legally."

She shook her head, her spiky hair tickling my chin. "The papers, the ones Sarah signed. They were at the house."

"Nope. I took them to a lawyer. She has them. I had a set of adoption papers she'd drawn up at the house. I'll have her do them again. File them, once we have our marriage license."

SAM

THE ROOM IN THE BASEMENT of the hospital seemed fitting. Everything was gray. The walls. Floor. Even the air seemed colored by it, the gloom gathering in corners like lost souls. I shivered and pressed closer to Easy's side. I wasn't poetic. Or fanciful. This was just a poorly-lit room with a large cooler set into one wall.

I should be grateful they hadn't buried Sarah in some nameless grave. Jane Doe #12. They didn't get many unidentified females here. A deputy and the coroner waited for us next to a stainless steel table. A sheet-draped body lay on it.

Easy squeezed my hand. I could do this. I had no choice. I inhaled deeply even as I realized Easy was barely breathing. His nostrils flared, and he breathed through his mouth in short little pants. Of course. Wolf senses. He could smell all the layers beneath the pine-scented cleanser. I'd expected the cloying sweet of death to coat my tongue when I breathed, but the fresh pine overwhelmed everything else.

"Ready, baby?"

His quiet question steadied me. "Yeah." I nodded to the coroner and spoke louder. "Let's get this done." My viewing Sarah's body was just a formality. Despite the differences beneath our skins, Sarah and I had been identical twins. The coroner recognized me the moment he saw me.

The coroner looked like a kind man, one who might carry peppermints in his pocket for his grandchildren. With evident respect for the dead, he folded the sheet across Sarah's chest, high enough to conceal the Y incision from her autopsy. I stepped closer, dropping Easy's hand in the process. He stood back, waiting, like he understood I had to do this alone.

All our lives, Sarah had searched for something. I'm not sure she even knew what it was. Her life hadn't been simple. Bad decisions. Bad people. A death at the hands of a man far more monstrous than the Wolf who waited four steps behind me, than the two other Wolves who waited outside. Digger and Hardy had accompanied us. If the Russian hadn't had club business to deal with, I suspect he would have been here as well.

Their presence filled an emptiness I'd only been vaguely aware of since I'd learned of Sarah's death. My sister was part of me, but she'd grown distant, putting space between us as if she'd foreseen her future and wanted me to accept her loss with less hurt. I studied her face, found her expression peaceful in death.

With a flash of understanding, I knew. Sarah *had* been waiting. Death was the solace she'd sought all along, but she couldn't leave her children. Couldn't leave me until she found someone to take care of us. That's why she'd taken Easy into her house, even knowing the trouble he'd bring. She instinctively knew. Somehow. Easy was mine. And by claiming me, he would claim the kids. And he would keep us safe. In his arms. In his heart. Protecting us from the monsters in the closet.

"That's her. That's my sister. Sarah Prescott." I swallowed and breathed. "Sarah Lucille Prescott."

"And your full name? For our records."

"Samantha Louise Prescott." I turned and smiled at Easy. "Cross. Samantha Louise Prescott Cross."

"Your sister never married?"

"Not really. It was a common law deal with her son's father that didn't last. She didn't give Jonah his father's last name."

I sat through the deputy's questions. We'd already concocted a story, much like the one Jonah told so he and Noni could get to Easy. I'm not sure the man truly believed me, but he couldn't shake my statement. Easy reinforced the idea that Sarah had gotten messed up with the Hell Dogs, and being the scum they were, they'd murdered her. I explained about the Bastard being Noni's father, which led to discussion about Jonah's.

The deputy verified the deaths of both, and though he gave Easy the fish eye, he signed off on his investigation and closed it.

We made arrangements to have Sarah cremated. We'd eventually take a trip with the kids to scatter her ashes where she could be truly free. Freedom shouldn't have been a new concept to me, but looking through my sister's tortured psyche, I found new understanding that rocked me.

Back at the clubhouse, Marie led me aside. The yard was already filling with people to celebrate my marriage to Easy. We did the justice-of-the-peace thing, but I was informed by the other old ladies that until the club celebrated, we weren't officially official. Marie made me laugh about it.

She was taking the kids to her place for a week so Easy and I could have a honeymoon. I worried about shuffling them around so much, but Marie and Deadhead had a girl and a boy the same ages as Jonah and Noni, and all four were best friends. Jonah was still too grown up for his age, but the Nightriders seemed determined to ensure he would enjoy the rest of his childhood. And Noni? I still couldn't get the picture of big, scary Gravedigger wearing a purple cape with a cardboard crown on his head having a picnic with a pink-tutu'd Noni out of my head.

The massive grill was fired up. Kegs

tapped. Music blared. The laughter of kids filtered through all the noise. Easy had given me so much, and I knew exactly what I was going to give him for a wedding present. Marie'd helped me choose my outfit. Short leather skirt, knee-high biker books, black lace tee shirt with a red bra and thong underneath. Even though I'd been wearing Easy's patch for awhile now, I was informed there was more involved. Meaning I couldn't wear my leather jacket until after. Good. I wanted Easy to know exactly what he was getting.

When the time came, the Russian appeared. He walked me to his bike, mounted, and I got on behind. Marie had told me this was a thing—that the president gave the bride away. I don't remember much after that. There were words. A leather vest that fit like a glove, and that wonderful leaping wolf patch and the words PROPERTY OF EASY on the back. Toasts. Bawdy advice. Food. Beer. People dancing and kissing. It was all a blur. All but the look in Easy's eyes when I walked up and took his hand. All but the crystalline purity of his love encompassing me.

EASY

WHEN SAM GOT OFF the Russian's bike, I thought I'd swallow my tongue. Legs. Her legs were magnificent under that scrap of leather she called a skirt. She flashed a hint of butt cheek, and I swear my dick was ready to rip through my jeans. I mumbled through the shit I was supposed to say, and Preacher laughed like a hyena at me. As soon as I put the cut I'd had made for Sam on her, I wanted to leave right then. Damn but I wanted to fuck my mate in the worst way.

I put up with everybody's crap until it was safe to leave. I'd made reservations at this fancy place down in the Ozarks. The honeymoon suite in a historic hotel. After all the crap Sam had survived, I wanted to spoil her. I could do all the frou-frou shit. Hell, for her I would have put on a fuckin' tux and stood in front of a church. Yeah, I was moonstruck. Bad.

My saddlebags were packed with a few days' worth of clothes. We wouldn't need many. I intended to keep Sam naked. In bed. In the bathtub. On the floor. On the fucking balcony. My dick was already planning all the ways we would fuck.

"Did you say goodbye to Noni?"

What? My plans screeched to a halt. "Noni? Yeah. She gave me attitude when I told her we had to leave."

"I'm not surprised. Did she refuse to give you a hug again? You know she's convinced that if she doesn't give you a hug, you can't leave, right?"

"Naw, I got a hug."

Sam pouted. "I didn't."

I hid my smirk. "Guess Noni figured out after the last time I walked out that the no-hugs method doesn't work on me."

Rolling her eyes, Sam climbed on behind me, slipped her arms around my waist and pressed her body along my back. Hot damn. If I hadn't cinched up my belt, my dick would be playing peek-a-boo with every car on the road.

At the first stoplight, Sam put her chin on my shoulder. "Where are you taking me?"

"Anywhere you want to go, baby."

"Good. Take the back roads."

Back roads? She blew into my ear, swiped her tongue along my jaw, and then bit me. "Jesus, woman. You're killin' me here. Taking the interstate, we're about four hours from our hotel. Why do you want me to take the back roads?"

I was damn proud of myself. Complete sentences came out of my mouth, and they even made sense.

"Because."

That sounded ominous. And sexy as hell. "Because?"

"Yes. I have a little wedding present for you."

The car behind us honked. I shot the driver the bird, but hit the throttle and roared off to the next stop light.

"What kinda present?"

"Remember that fantasy you had?"

Fantasy? Hell, I'd had hundreds of them. "Uh..." My brain quit sending words to my mouth as all of them converged at once and my head hit overload.

"The one about your motorcycle...ring a bell?"

I swallowed. Hard. My dick was knocking on my belt.

"Yeah...and?"

"Take the back roads, Easy, because I'm going to ride you full throttle."

"Oh fuck, baby."

We did. I hit a road with no traffic and stopped long enough for her to unbutton my jeans, free my aching dick, and mount the front of my bike facing me. That's when I discovered she was wearing only a thong. I ripped that sucker in a heartbeat and thrust inside her. She screamed, her eyes wild as I revved the bike.

I popped the clutch, and we took off. The vibrations from that powerful shovelhead engine throbbed through us both. She used those athletic legs of hers to squeeze my thighs, rising and falling in a ride wilder than any I'd ever experienced.

"Fuckin' A, Sam. I'm so damn close. Come with me, baby. Come with me now!"

Her fingers gripped my shoulders, and she shuddered. Her climax flooded my dick with wet heat, and I shot my load, pumping endlessly into her. She kissed me, squeezed my dick with her inner muscles and then laughed.

She threw back her head and screamed to the stars, "I love you so damn much my heart can't hold it all. I have to shout it to the world. I LOVE YOU!" She kissed me again and then curled around me, arms and legs, keeping us joined. "I know now what it means. All of it. I'm alive, Easy. We're alive and free."

"And nobody can ever take it away from us, baby."

The black ribbon of highway stretched out in front of us. The stars and moon watched from the sky. I'd found my mate, and we had the rest of our lives.

"Alive and free, baby. Always."

Dear Readers:

While "living" in the world of my Moonstruck Wolves, I discovered a darker underbelly. My secret (and slightly guilty) love of MC books might have had something to do with my detour into the gritty, violent lives of the Nightriders. These outlaw MC brothers roared out of the dark into my imagination, and above the growl of their Harleys, I heard each of their distinct voices. As a result, I'm trying something new to me— writing their stories in first person.

The story Easy and Sam told me went places dark, dangerous, and violent. It won't be for everyone. Easy is a criminal. His Nightrider brothers are criminals. And their enemies, the Hell Dogs, think nothing of rape, torture, and murder. If readers are sensitive to these themes, this is not the book for them.

As an author, I'm always humbled when readers love my characters as much as I do. I live with these people during the course of their stories. They are very real to me and to know that they come alive in readers' imaginations leaves me gobsmacked. Thank you.

Again, thank you for visiting my worlds. The door is always open so don't be a stranger. Happy reading!

~Silver James

Thank you for reading NIGHT SHIFT. I hope you enjoyed it. Reviews help other readers find books to read. I appreciate every review, good or bad. Please consider leaving one at Amazon or on Goodreads. If this is your first book set in the Moonstruck world, please check out other books set there, and my other books, too.

Coming soon –
Another New Series set in the world of Moonstruck

Hard Target
Double Cross – Book 1

MOONSTRUCK
The Award-winning Series

MOONSTRUCK: SECRETS

The existence of Wolves has remained a secret for over 200 years. Now, the members of Army Special SciOps Unit 69 are about to be exposed. When a covert operation behind enemy lines goes wrong, Sergeant Major Ian McIntire must trust Major Hannah Jackson to save his men—and his heart. She's already privy most of his secrets but the one she doesn't know about the moonstruck alpha werewolf may get them all killed. She has one chance to get them undercover and safe, but it may already be too late.

Ten years later, former Army sniper Michael Lightfoot's life as a forest ranger fits his need to run wild when the moon is full—until two wild wolf pups are kidnapped, along with Dr. Liz Graham, the wildlife biologist who makes him want to howl. The last thing he expects when he rescues the feisty doctor is to be moonstruck. With her life in danger, he must reveal his true self—and risk losing her—in order to save her from the shady corporation stalking the Wolves.

Warning: Secrets, lies, and betrayals are more personal under the full moon, but when a Wolf loves a woman, he'll do whatever it takes to keep her safe.

Welcome back to the Moonstruck world with this first full length Moonstruck novel containing new and deleted scenes in addition to the first two novellas, BLOOD MOON and BAD MOON.

Note:

Still Available – the original novellas (In digital only)

Blood Moon
(Moonstruck –Book 1)

Army Major Hannah Jackson knows where the skeletons are hidden at the

Pentagon and now she's been tasked with keeping the secrets of Army Special Sci Ops Unit 69—the Wolves—and their secret is a doozy. That a civilian corporation wants to exploit the Wolves is a matter of pressing concern.

Sergeant Major Ian McIntire doesn't trust Hannah as far as he can throw her—and that's quite a ways considering he's an alpha werewolf. The woman is a pain in his butt and with the Blood Moon coming, the unit needs to complete their mission and get home before tempers flare. While she might know most of their secrets, the one she doesn't know about the moonstruck Wolf might just get them all killed.

When a covert operation goes wrong, Mac must trust Hannah to save his men—and his heart. Secrets, lies, and betrayals are more personal under the full moon, but when a Wolf loves a woman, he'll do whatever it takes to keep her safe.

Warning: Pursue an alpha Wolf at your own risk. Hot sex, bad words, and action of the blood and guts kind will ensue.

WINNER 2013 INTERNATIONAL DIGITAL AWARDS SHORT PARANORMAL NOVEL

Bad Moon
(Moonstruck –Book 2)

Former Army sniper Michael Lightfoot lives a simple life as a forest ranger in Wyoming. The job fits his need to run wild when the moon is full—until two special wolf pups are kidnapped, along with Dr. Liz Graham, the wildlife biologist who makes him want to howl.

The last thing Michael expects when he meets the feisty doctor is to be moonstruck, but the alpha Wolf has more on his plate than just convincing Dr. Liz to love him for who he is. She's being stalked by mercenaries who stole two wolf pups for an unknown faction. Now, with her life in danger, he must reveal his true self to save her. Reuniting with some of his old Army Special SciOps unit, Michael takes on the corporate raiders who want more than just his hide—and Liz's expertise.

Secrets, lies, and betrayals are more personal under the full moon, but when a Wolf loves a woman, he'll risk heart and soul to keep her.

Warning: When a moonstruck Wolf meets his mate, hot sex will ensue. If his mate is threatened, bad words and violence of the blood and guts variety will definitely occur.

Hunter's Moon
(Moonstruck –Book 3)

Dr. Jacey Randolph just might be crazy. A rescued wolf is more than he seems and his ability to get into her head—literally—makes her doubt her sanity. After the death of her husband in the Gulf War, she returned to the family ranch to run an animal sanctuary. Bad enough she has to fend off advances from the local sheriff, but now she's turning into some sort of Dr. Doolittle. Except she doesn't talk to animals, dammit.

When Colonel Joshua Harjo, an old friend of her husband's, shows up on her doorstep with a wild tale that the wolf is actually Marine Captain Nathaniel Connor, Jacey must make a leap of faith—and jeopardize her heart—to get involved with the wolf and a group of former Army SciOps soldiers in full rescue operation mode.

Secrets, lies, and betrayals are more personal under the full moon but when a woman loves a Wolf, he can do no wrong. And Jacey Randolph is not about to let a little thing like a band of mercenaries keep her from the Wolf she loves.

Warning: Explosions, death, and sex go hand in hand when a group of Wolves and their women fight for their existence.

Wolf Moon
(Moonstruck Book 4)

Sean Donaldson, former combat medic and demolition expert, answers an SOS from an old Army buddy and rides smack dab into the middle of a conspiracy. Murder and kidnapping are just the tip of the iceberg. Going undercover with a biker gang seems the quickest solution but Sean's best intentions are complicated by Annie Simmons and her son, Cody.

Annie is a waitress at the Half Dollar Bar and Grill just scraping by to provide a better life for her son. She doesn't want a man in her life, especially a scary dude like "Boomer," the big biker who steals a part of her heart. What she doesn't know about the lies he's told can hurt her…and put Cody in danger.

Secrets, lies, and betrayals are more personal under the full moon but when a Wolf fights for his heart, he'll risk his life to make sure the family he loves survives.

Warning: When it's the month of the Wolf Moon, anybody who gets between a moonstruck Wolf and his mate deserves what they get. Blood, sex, and four-letter words dead ahead.

Bride's Moon
(Moonstruck Book 5)

When the remnants of Special SciOps Unit 69, the Wolves, reunited to save a group of soldiers used as lab rats in a secret experiment, Colonel Joshua Harjo never expected to command the covert government unit again. Someone near the top wants the 69th back on active duty and Harjo is tasked with making it happen, along with keeping the men the Wolves rescued top secret.

Amy Rouse is the best "cat herder" around and she's recruited for administrative duties with the new unit, a job with perks—Wolves and their commanding officer, Joshua Hargo, the man of her dreams. Amy didn't count on murder, mayhem, and a redheaded Deputy US Marshal to complicate her life.

Secrets, lies, and betrayals are more personal under the full moon, but when a man loves a woman, nothing will stop him from tying the knot.

Warning: The road to romance is never smooth and a runaway bride might just jinx a highly sensitive operation.

Rogue Moon
(Moonstruck Book 6)

Rudek Tornjak is a Wolf without a pack. A man scarred by his past, he prefers it that way. While living in the shadows of the

French Quarter, whispers of treachery and betrayal reach his ears—along with accusations implicating him in unthinkable acts. He comes out of hiding to confront his accusers only to discover he's under a death sentence. On the run, he encounters Isabelle Fontaine, a woman with a past of her own she'd rather keep hidden.

Family is everything to Izzy and she'll do whatever it takes to keep hers safe. Crossing paths with a shadowy corporation and a rogue Wolf puts the people she cares about in jeopardy—not to mention her own life and heart.

Secrets, lies, and betrayals are more personal under the full moon, but when a betrayed Wolf fights for his honor, no one is safe—not even the woman he loves.

Warning: Doubt a Wolf's honor and you'll get a serving of hot blood and guts to go.

Christmas Moon
(A Moonstruck Novella)

The Wolves have been busy since blowing up half of Louisiana. Thanks to the government, there's a bounty on their heads so they're living off the grid. But Christmas is here and the kids want to know if Santa will find them this year. Not a problem until the phone call asking them to find and rescue a pregnant girl. On December 20th. In New Mexico. Piece of fruit cake, right?

Walking into a firefight with a drug cartel is never easy, but with Hannah's wrath and Liam's first change on the line, Mac and the Wolves face a harder choice—save the girl or save Christmas.

Secrets, lies, and betrayals are more personal under the Christmas moon, and it might just take the magic of Santa to help the Wolves save the day and make it home to their families in time. Because in the end, it's all about family.

Warning: Santa's making his list and when the Wolves go into action, they'll find out who's naughty and who's nice.

FINALIST 2014 INTERNATIONAL DIGITAL AWARDS SHORT PARANORMAL NOVEL

Blue Moon
(Moonstruck Book 8)

DJ Collier is a manhunter. As a Deputy US Marshal, she'll go after any fugitive, but the names in the secret file dumped on her desk must be ghosts considering the lack of information she can gather. Where better to hunt them than in the last place she encountered the elusive group of military Special Operators? She never expected to find death, destruction, and a sexy Wolf determined to make her his in the Louisiana bayous.

Antoine Fontaine has lived in the bayous all his life. Always standing on the outside of his close-knit Cajun family, he thinks he's one of a kind. He never expected to discover another like himself, much less a whole group of SpecOps Wolves who welcome him into their pack. He has no idea what it means to be moonstruck until he rescues a feisty Deputy US Marshal. Now, he'll fight to the death to keep her.

Once in a Blue Moon, a Wolf finds his mate and even if he's up to his ass in alligators, he'll keep her safe. Warning: Hot sex, explosions, and mayhem of the blood and guts kind dead ahead.

Moon Shot
(Moonstruck Book 9)
A Moonstruck/Hard Target Crossover Novel)

Scorched earth. The Wolves are damn tired of being hunted. They've licked their wounds and now it's time to take the fight to the enemy. They're moving on up—all the way to the hallowed halls of government. Intelligence reports indicate their enemies are getting closer—and more personal. Assassination of the Wolves and their families is on the menu and SEAL Team Atlantis has the kill order.

Unexpected allies, a new baby, and the healing of old wounds give the Wolves something to live—and fight—for. Every last one of them is ready for a Happy Ever After.

Retribution. There are three things a Wolf holds sacred—his mate, his pups, and his pack. Threaten any one of them and you'd better be checking your six. Threaten all three? Just remember—secrets, lies, and betrayals demand payback and the Wolves are ready to hunt.

Warning: Wolves don't hold a grudge, they get even.

The Exciting Urban Fantasy Series
The Penumbra Papers
Cases from the Shadow's Edge
Penumbra: Etymology: New Latin, from Latin paene almost + umbra shadow

These "Cases from the Shadow's Edge" explore the forces of light and dark as they dance through shadows humans barely glimpsed prior to the Big Rip. Since then, all manner of preternatural magicks intermingle with humans in ways mysterious, magical and, in some cases, criminal. Much to humanity's surprise, there really are monsters under the bed and the things that go bump in the night are bigger and scarier than anyone ever imagined.

Vampires. Ghouls. Faeries. Ghosts. Werewolves. Creatures of legend and nightmares. Overnight, reality took on a whole new meaning. The world's best and brightest from every discipline—physics, theology, anthropology, chemistry, to name only a few—all tried to explain the rip in the cosmic curtain. Sade Marquis has her own theory. The monsters have been here all along, flying just under the radar of normal perception. They've been masquerading as mundanes—their term for humans. Of course, Sade knows the truth of the matter. She was raised by a master vampire and her pet "dog" shifted into a boy the night of her twelfth birthday. Sade's very good at keeping secrets. She has a lot of them.

This is where *Special Agent* Sade Marquis enters the mix. A human FBI agent with an X-Files mentality, Sade's been handpicked to fill a new slot within the Bureau— Preternatural Liaison Officer with the MAGIC Unit. The Magical Activity, Grievances, and Inhuman Crimes unit is in charge of investigations involving magicks. It's her job to deal with all the monsters, and she's very, very good at her job. That makes the magicks very, very afraid of her. As they should be...

That Ol' Black Magic
Penumbra Papers #0.5

Along with her FBI partner—and werewolf best friend—Caleb Jones, Sade is sent to New Orleans to investigate the murders of several high-ranking magicks. The Big Easy is neutral territory so Sade must find and arrest the culprit before war breaks out between the Realms. Things look up when the gargoyle Sentinel, Roman, a permanent fixture in Sade's childhood, arrives to keep the peace. Maybe.

The investigation is hampered by Sade's faerie nemesis, Ariel—the King's Seducer. Oh, and then there's the new dragon in town, Nikolas Constantine. Sade can't decide whether to arrest his ass or admire it.

When guilt and innocence come to play in the French Quarter, it'll take Sade's brand of crazy to sort it all out.

WINNER 2014 INTERNATIONAL DIGITAL AWARDS SHORT PARANORMAL NOVEL

Season Of The Witch
Penumbra Papers #1

Sade Marquis. Her best friend turns furry. Her godfather is a master vampire. Her mother was once the mistress of Oberon, King of the Faerie Court.

When the Veil between the mortal and magical realms rips, FBI Special Agent Sade Marquis is in a unique position to head up the newly-formed MAGIC unit. She's the only human who knows exactly what goes bump in the night. When things go to hell in a handbasket and there's magic in the air, Sade is the agent FBI Director George Bailey wants in the trenches. She's savvy, snarky, and sexy but she may have met her match when she's sent to Chicago to investigate the murder of a congressional aide.

Is the vampire, Kristian St. John, guilty as sin? Once a Templar knight, Sinjen now teaches history at the University of Chicago. He must rely on Sade to clear his name and track the real culprit.

Together, they unravel the clues to a mystery that began a thousand years before. If they don't solve the murders of six young women, the whole world—human *and* magick—will suffer the evil consequences.

FINALIST 2014 INTERNATIONAL DIGITAL AWARDS LONG PARANORMAL NOVEL

From Harlequin Desire:
Red Dirt Royalty
These Oklahoma millionaires work hard and play harder!

Cowgirl's Don't Cry
The wealthiest of enemies may seduce the ranch right out from under her!

Cassidy Morgan wasn't raised a crybaby. So when her father dies and leaves the family ranch vulnerable to takeover by an Okie gazillionaire with a grudge, she doesn't shed a tear—she fights back.

But Chance Barron, the son of said gazillionaire, is a too-sexy adversary. In fact, it isn't until Cassidy falls head over heels for the sexy cowboy-hat-wearing attorney that she even finds out he's the enemy. Now she needs a plucky plan to save her birthright. But Chance has another trick up his sleeve, putting family loyalties—and passion—to the ultimate test.

The Cowgirl's Little Secret
She's back at his ranch...with baby in tow.

When nurse Jolie Davis comes home, she knows it's only a matter of time before she runs into Cord Barron—the Barrons own this town. In fact, it was their oil business rivalry with her father that caused her break up with Cord in the first place. But no amount of family meddling can deny the fact that she had his secret son. Now, four years later, as her ex is wheeled into the ER—while she's on duty!—it's time to come clean. Because it quickly becomes clear that Cord is determined to reclaim her...

Also Coming Soon:

The Full-length Moonstruck Novels
Moonstruck: Secrets
Moonstruck: Lies
Moonstruck: Betrayal
Moonstruck: Retribution

Penumbra Papers
The Devil's Cut

Two New Series from Silver James

Nightriders MC
Night Shift – Book 1

Hard Target
Double Cross – Book 1

Acknowledgements

Writing is the one profession where the voices in my head mean I'm only a little crazy when I talk back to them. I love my voices, even when they argue with me. Which they do. Way more than they should. Silly buggers.

As always, many thanks to the Wild Warriors on my street team, friends, and family. Y'all are the reason I keep writing the stories in my head.

I truly appreciate the help I receive from my critique partner Heidi, beta reader Siobhan, and cover artist Clary for the many "do-overs" until we get things right. I couldn't write anything remotely military without the help and guidance of my wonderful husband, Greg aka Lawyer Guy. I also want to thank author Jill Sorenson for a fantastic class on writing MC romances, and an old friend who didn't patch in but knows many who did.

Last but definitely not least, I want to recognize my readers. Each email, Facebook comment, tweet, and visit to my website convinces me that I must be doing something right.

One last caveat: Any and all mistakes are my own.

About the Author

Silver likes walking on the wild side and coffee. Okay. She loves coffee. LOTS of coffee. Warning: Her Muse, Iffy, runs with scissors and can be quite dangerous. An award-winning author, she's been a military officer's wife, mother, state appellate court marshal, airport rescue firefighter and forensic fire photographer, crime analyst, technical crime scene investigator, and writer of magic and mystery. Now retired from the "real world," she lives in Oklahoma and spends her days at the computer with two Newfoundland dogs, the cat who rules them all, and myriad characters all clamoring for attention. She writes dark urban fantasy thrillers, time travel romance, and sexy contemporary romance.

To find out more about Silver and her books, visit her website:

www.silverjames.com.

She loves to connect with readers on Facebook and Twitter.

Titles by Silver James:

Moonstruck:
*Blood Moon – Book 1
*Bad Moon – Book 2
*Hunter's Moon – Book 3
*Wolf Moon – Book 4
*Bride's Moon – Book 5
*Rogue Moon – Book 6
*Christmas Moon (A Moonstruck Novella #7)
*Blue Moon – Book 8
*Moon Shot – Book 9 (A Moonstruck/Hard Target Crossover Novel)
Moonstruck: Secrets

Nightriders MC:
Night Shift (Nightriders MC #1)

Hard Target
Double Cross (Hard Target #1)

Penumbra Papers:
That Ol' Black Magic
Season of the Witch
The Devil's Cut

Other Novella:
*Café Midnight

From Harlequin Desire
Red Dirt Royalty
Cowgirls Don't Cry
The Cowgirl's Little Secret

From the Wild Rose Press:
Faerie Fate
Faerie Fire
Faerie Fool
*Faerie Faith (Twelve Brides of Christmas)
(novella)
*Faerie Reign (Boxed set containing the three
full-length novels at a special price)

Class of '85 Reunion Series:
*Fairy Tales Can Come True
*Promises, Promises

Dearly Beloved Series:
*Best Laid Plans

*Available in digital format only